KU-735-986

Other books by Melvin Burgess

MELVIN BURGESS

Sara's Face

ANDERSEN PRESS • LONDON

For my daughter, Pearl

This edition first published in 2017 by
Andersen Press Limited
20 Vauxhall Bridge Road
London SW1V 2SA
www.andersenpress.co.uk

2 4 6 8 10 9 7 5 3 1

First published in hardback by Andersen Press Ltd in 2006

Text copyright © Melvin Burgess, 2006, 2008

British Library Cataloguing in Publication Data available.

ISBN 978 1 78344 488 5

Printed and bound in Great Britain by Clays Limited,
Bungay, Suffolk, NR35 1ED

Introduction

Just about everyone knows the story of Jonathon Heat and Sara Carter. It's common currency, revealed to us through a thousand newspaper headlines, magazine articles, news bulletins, TV shows and an endless commentary on the radio. Heat's sheer celebrity is one factor that made the story of such universal interest. While he still had one, his was perhaps the most famous face on the planet. We've been hearing about him for years but the strange nature of his crimes and his terrible fate have made this particular story his most lasting legacy to us.

Sara is different. She comes down to us as a mystery, a figure without explanation. Her refusal or inability to speak has led to endless speculation about her, but the story of her hopes and dreams, and her role in the terrible way they were fulfilled, remain elusive. How much did she plan? Was she in control the whole time, or was she just the innocent victim of Heat and his surgeon, Wayland Kaye? It's the purpose of this book to try to cast some light on the girl herself.

As someone used to trying to create an impression of truth, investigating actual truth has proved to be a tricky affair. Both Heat and Sara seem to have been master dissemblers themselves, with only very shaky ideas of who they really were or what they wanted to become. Heat, of course, is in prison. Sara's fate is more open to speculation. Since her failure to come and give evidence in court, rumours have circulated widely; madness or death, or the terrible nature of her injuries, seem to be the most likely options, but, to this day, no one is really sure. I'm a novelist doing a journalist's job, and my brief has been to get at what people thought and felt, and what their motivations were, as much as simply to describe the unfolding of events. What goes on in people's hearts is a notoriously tricky thing to know. I've done my best to understand rather than speculate, but, frankly, I've been amazed at how little positive truth you come across after even the most thorough investigation. Everything that happens is filtered through opinion and memory, and of course by how much other people want you to know. No two people remember anything in exactly the same way. I've done my best to verify, everything before I came to write it. Most of all, I've done my best to be true to Sara.

I've been able to speak to almost all the people involved in the events that took place in Cheshire in 2005, except of course the two main protagonists. Even with all the contacts in my hand, Sara has proved to be incredibly elusive. She told so many different versions of what was going on to so many different people, it's as if she has done her best to

2

extinguish her real self in favour of her own legend. Perhaps that's the nature of her tragedy. Like a religious figure or a character from myth, it's nothing she ever said or did but her story itself that forces her on our attention and inspires our imagination. In that sense, she more than achieved her ambition of making fame itself a work of art.

There is one great asset I've been given access to, however – the video diary that Sara kept on and off over the years, including during her stay at Home Manor Farm. This may be the only chance we will ever have of hearing her speak directly to us again, so let's start off with that right away. Here she is talking about her boyfriend, Mark, a few days before she went into the hospital where she first met Jonathon Heat.

Sara — 2 April 2005

(Sara is sitting in a chair looking off to the side of the camera, as if someone else is sitting there talking to her. But hers is the only voice we hear. In fact, she's pretending to be interviewed for the TV. Occasionally she glances at the camera and examines something — she can probably see herself on a monitor. At other times, she forgets where she is and seems to be talking almost to herself. It's as if she's working out her own thoughts and feelings through this pretend interview.)

No, that's not true. I did love him, I really did. I still do. But it has to *work*. Love isn't the same as compatibility, I've had to learn that. It's a hard lesson. You'd think love would be enough. Mark was too different from me. It had to stop.

(She pauses as if she's being asked a question.)

Well, we seemed to get along so well, but in the end we're actually perfect opposites. He thinks, like, the sensible people are the ones who have it sorted. Like *they're* going to inherit the earth. *(Laughs.)* Like sensible *is it*. Anything you do that's important, it has to be sensible, that's Mark, whereas me, I want everything I do that's important to be unexpected – just about ready to bend everything sideways.

I used to scare him, I think. 'You'll get hurt,' he used to say, but maybe what he really meant was, he'd get hurt. He used to talk about it as if it had already happened. I mean – as if he could sit down and work out the future with a pencil and paper. You don't work out the future! The future works you out. To see the future you have to be able to prophesy, and it's not the sensible ones who can do that – it's the people who don't know what on earth is going on, the ones who know absolutely nothing, who can see into the future and see ghosts and that. I've done it. I may talk about it one day. He wants to make sure he has enough pants packed for the journey through life. Well, I might not even be wearing any pants at all. You think I know fuck all, but I know fuck nothing – that's me. I don't know who I am, I don't even know what I am. That's how I can see into the future. That's how sensible I am!

(She laughs, as delighted with her own words as if they had been spoken by someone else. She leans forward to the hidden monitor and fixes her hair, then leans back and sighs.)

Stick to the flesh, boy! I am the spirit.

He's the flesh all right, though. He does my head in sometimes, I want him so much. That's what I miss most. Being close. He's someone you can get very close to.

(Sara looks down and fiddles with her shirt, frowning as if she's forgotten where she is.)

We were lying on the sofa at his flat. We'd just been busy. Busy bees, we call it. I was lying there with a skirt on and just about nothing else and he had my T-shirt rolled up and he was sort of adoring my boobs. Boob adoration.

'Gorgeous. Like puppies. Like warm little puppies with hot pink noses,' he was saying, and he kept giving me goose flesh by breathing on them.

'Well, make the most of them, they won't be around much longer,' I told him.

'What do you mean, you're not going to put them away, are you?' he said. *(Laughs.)* He makes me laugh; I'll forgive him anything for making me laugh. I miss that about him, too. Yeah! A boy has to make me laugh!

'I've started saving up,' I told him. He knew what I meant. I was serious. I wanted to tell him because he's my boyfriend. He's involved. I mean, he ought to be my soul mate or something, but that's too much to ask from someone who's only sensible.

I knew we were going to have a row about it.

'You ought to be grateful I've got my clothes on – it's such a mess underneath. Talk about cellulite. It's revolting. This tit's practically under my arm when I lie down. What good's that on a photo shoot?'

'They use tit tape for that,' he told me.

'Tit tape! I want to look like that naturally; anyone can use tit tape. And this one's bigger than that one, they both point sideways when I stand up and anyway – mostly, they're just too small and the wrong shape. They've got to go. I need new tits. I need a whole new body, actually. I get fatter when I'm dieting. I get fat just by breathing. I can turn air into fat. It's a gift I have.'

(She giggles at her own words.)

You should have seen his face! Like I was taking away his favourite toy car or something.

'You can't do that! They're mine,' he said.

I said, 'They're just on loan, buddy, and don't you forget it.'

He says they're lovely, but he's just saying that to be nice, I think. 'How can anything be better?' he says, but plenty of things are better than them. Too many things are better, that's the problem.

Up until that point it was just fun, but then he started to get all serious on me. 'You know what they do to you when you get that done?' he said. 'They cut you here, right round the nipple. They get it out on a stalk, man! They get your nipple on a stalk while they stitch bags inside your tits – it's like torture. And then you know what? You lose feeling. They cut loads of nerves doing that and they never grow back. Sex will never be as good again.'

'I don't care,' I told him. I mean, if you want to be a work of art, you have to suffer a bit. That's all part of the package. But he pissed me off then, going on about blood and cutting and things. That's not what I wanted to hear.

We used to argue a lot, about everything. It was fun at first, it was like a game; we'd make out that the other one was being weird. But then it got like I'm weird and he's just pretending. Like it's dawned on him that it's not just a game. He says he loves me. Baby! I got no time for love. Christ, I'm seventeen – I'm just practising. Love, what's that? I'm an obsessive, personally. Passion! He thinks he means so much to me. I don't know.

So that thing about my tits, it went on to be a big row. I wanted to discuss with him what sort of op I was going to have. I wanted him to have some input, you know? I mean, your girlfriend wants to discuss her boobs with you, she actually wants to know what sort of tits you want her to have – she's actually offering you a chance to help design the perfect tits and all you do is go on at her! What's that about? What is he on? Who's the weird one, you tell me? Doesn't he know a good deal when it's handed to him on a plate? I offer him a dream ticket and he starts telling me what I can and what I can't do with my own tits?!

(She grabs hold of them with both hands. She looks outraged.)

My own tits! So that was it. I'd had enough. Tenancy over. Pack your bags and go. It really hurt me, but what else could I do? I hurt myself sometimes. He was heartbroken, too, at least that's how he made out. Just another week, give me a chance, it was just a joke, he said. But it had been going on too long. Every time I talked about my ambitions he'd get jealous and try to talk some sense into me. Well, that's just about abuse to someone like me, having someone force sense down your throat.

I miss him, I do miss him. But, let's face it, I gave him another chance. There he was – begging for another week, just one more week, give us one last chance, so I let him have it and then, guess what? I never see him again! I tell him OK and he leaves me! What's that about?

(She swallows back her tears and gets angry instead.)

Like it was him that couldn't be bothered! That's so mean. And now I expect he's sitting somewhere waiting for me to get back in touch. I expect he's breaking his heart for me, but fuck him. He humiliated me. No one treats me like that and gets away with it. If I never see him again, it'll be too soon.

So that's why I wrote a song for him that I'm going to sing for you tonight, about what a shit he was to me, so the whole world's gonna know what he's like.

(She produces a guitar from behind her chair and sings.)

> Mark Gleeson is a big shit,
> Mark Gleeson is a big shit,
> Mark Gleeson is a big shit, fuck him.
> His telephone number is 0161 352 7980.
> Ring him up and tell him what a shit he is.
> He broke my heart,
> He broke my heart and made me cry.

(*Cries.*)

But I'll get over it. I'm going to be famous. (*Wiping away her tears.*) I made up my mind about it, there's no point in trying to talk me out of it. Art on legs, Mark used to say, but that's not what I mean. People say I'm good-looking like that, but there's loads of girls prettier than me, or sexier than me or whatever. That's not the point. Anyone can be pretty these days. Anyone can have nice tits and a pretty face. Talent – that's not it, either. Anyone can have talent. They train you up, they work on your voice. If it's no good they change it in the studio. The world's full of talent. Talent's cheap.

It's like, when people look at you and think, Oh, she's smaller than in real life, because, see, actually, you're not real life. It's when people start talking to you in the street or on the bus because they think they know you, but they've never even met you, or like you've got some secret that they want to know but they never can. Like you're a blessing. There's something about you that inspires them to be more than themselves. That's it. That's what I want to be. Just like that.

Some people want to be famous so everyone knows who they are. They don't get it. It's not about who knows you or who you are. It's about being more than who you are. It's not what you do – it's what you make other people do. I mean, I'm famous even when no one's looking. I'm famous even before I'm famous. I want it so when people look at me they think things they've never thought before – they think things they never even knew they were capable of thinking. It's art. You look at it, and maybe it annoys the hell out of you because you can never understand it. Maybe there's nothing to understand, but it's fascinating anyway. And all the time, right on the edge of your mind, there's thoughts lurking like wild animals, and feelings you never felt. You can't work them out, you don't know if it's monsters or angels and you're frightened of understanding because they might just burst out and change your whole life. Your whole life! Yeah. That's me. Your whole life!

Mark used to say I'm a wannabe, but I say, I'm a gonnabe. That's the difference.

I know. I'm arrogant. But it's true what I say, I can't help it. It's in my bones. And he could have been there with me. Now look at him. He just got left behind.

(She stares into the camera with a frightened expression. Then she catches sight of her expression and raises a hand to the lens.)

Cut.

(She wipes away her tears and turns off the camera.)

Voices

Sara seems to have been a very popular girl while she was at primary school and stayed that way for the first couple of years at high school. After that, her popularity wavered. Some people thought she was just plain weird, others that her behaviour was put on for effect. Either way, she was too strong a taste for many of her contemporaries, but those who did love her loved her dearly and were loved in return. Even when she rose beyond them, she never forgot who her friends were, or what friendship meant to her.

Sara and Janet Calley met each other in their first year at high school and that was it – they were friends for life. For a couple of years they did everything together: ran around the corridors giggling at the same jokes, read the same books, sometimes even wore the same clothes. Anyone who saw them would have thought of them as two peas in a pod, but Janet already knew that Sara was altogether different. When in Year 9 Sara suddenly turned into a different person, she wasn't in the least bit surprised.

Sara shot up. In a few months, she grew over thirty centimetres. Her figure, which seemed to have been holding puberty at bay so far, suddenly bloomed. After a brief spell of acne her face healed in a few weeks into the clearest skin, without a blemish and so finely grained that not a pore was visible to the naked eye. Her flawless skin was one of the things that attracted the attention of Jonathon Heat, who had always had an open complexion.

At the same time she developed a scent all of her own.

'I noticed it on her one day,' said Janet, 'and I asked her what she was wearing.'

'Can you smell it, too?' she asked. 'It's not anything. I didn't even wash this morning.'

They were both astonished by this trick of nature and went to lock themselves in the toilet so they could smell the skin on her arms, her legs, on her back and shoulders, and verify that it was her skin all over. It was true. She smelt all over of salted almonds and musk.

'She never had to wear deodorant, after a shower,' said Janet, shaking her head in amazement. 'I never came across anything like it. Her own perfume! She used to say she was fed up with it, she'd like to smell of something else, but, really, she was very proud to be her own perfume. They could have made a fortune if they ever put it in a bottle.'

As a result of her height and her looks, Sara suddenly began to attract a great deal of attention from boys, which she suffered with a kind of bemused tolerance, always keeping them at arm's length. Later, when her face was known across the world, the newspapers tried to make out that she slept with a great many of those boys. Janet always maintained that it wasn't true.

'She wasn't like that at all. In fact, she used to have this joke about how she was going to be the last virgin on earth, because she was still holding out when all the rest of us were already at it. But I suppose it's her own fault. She liked it that people thought that about her. I had to promise not to tell anyone she was a virgin, although, actually, she was very proud and wanted only to do it with someone special.'

'It'd be bad for my image if people knew,' she said. In fact, Sara was a virgin right up until she met Mark, a little after her seventeenth birthday, and, as far as Janet's aware, she never slept with anyone else.

When the sexual attention got out of hand, Sara put a stop to it in a way that won a great deal of disapproval from her classmates. It happened like this.

It had started as a game of chase years before at primary school. The old story – the boys chase the girls and rough them up or put their hands under their clothes. The game had died down at high school, when people didn't know each other so well, but a small group of boys and girls had started it up again sometime in Year 8. They were good friends, all five of them, and spent time together out of school as well as in it. The three boys would pounce on one of the girls, drag her into the boys' cloakroom and have a quick grope with much shrieking and howls of laughter.

The girls enjoyed it as much as the boys, but there's a fine line between rough play and bullying, and another again

14

between bullying and sexual assault. It wasn't quite childish any more and it wasn't just chase. Once or twice, the boys tried it on someone else and just about got away with it. Their fatal mistake was trying it with Sara. Sara was friendly with these boys – not close, just friendly. She was the most desirable girl in the school and it's a sign that more than fun or curiosity was involved that they tried it on with her. One day, as they were walking with her past the cloakrooms, they pounced, dragged her off out of sight and rummaged inside her clothes.

Janet was standing outside with another girl when it happened. She stood and listened to the boys grunting with laughter and Sara's shrieks of indignity, her heart beating furiously. It wasn't Sara she was worried about. The boys were going places they weren't welcome but she was in no danger – it wasn't real violence.

'They didn't ought to be doing that,' said the girl next to her. Janet remembers thinking how right she was.

It was over in a few seconds. The boys came running out, giggling and smirking, and Sara came staggering after them, tucking her shirt in. She walked up to Janet, whipped out her mobile phone and dialled. She stared straight at them as she spoke.

'Police.'

The corridor, which had been abuzz a moment before, suddenly froze.

'I've just been sexually assaulted in the boys' toilets at Stanford High School by a group of three boys. My name's Sara Carter; I have the boys here. I'm with some friends so it's safe. There are witnesses. Please send a squad car round as soon as possible.'

She stabbed the phone and started another dial-up.

'It was just a laugh,' said one of them.

'You can't do that,' said another.

'She wasn't even dialling,' said the third.

She didn't answer them. 'Hello. Can I have the news desk? My name is Sara Carter and I've just been sexually assaulted at Stanford High School. The police are on their way. Three boys. Yes. I'm only thirteen years old.'

'Bollocks,' said Barry. They were all looking really scared.

'It's a game, right?' said Joey.

Then she rang the Head. He was in a meeting at the time, so she spoke to his secretary. 'Tell him to get his arse over here, the boys' toilets near the maths block. This is Sara Carter and I've just been molested by some pupils from this school. The police and the press are already on their way.'

She turned off her phone and stared at the boys.

'Watch me,' she said. She crumpled up her face and began to cry.

'Oh my God,' said Barry Jones. By the time the Head came running down the corridor with members of staff around him like a herd of rhinos, they knew it was real.

'It's them,' said Sara. 'They nearly raped me,' she said – which wasn't true. 'They touched me,' she said, which was. Then she burst into tears. Above the shouting and cries of complaint, they could hear the squad car howling in through the school gates.

And all hell broke loose. The school, the press, the police, everything. The drama was played out in full public view, like so much of her life to come. The boys were arrested as the press cameras flashed; the Head granted a desperate interview while the police overacted for the film crew. The story, as Sara had realised at once, was a beauty. It hit the local TV news that evening and was all over the papers the next day. Gang of teenage boys attempt rape of girl, 13, in school toilets. Fabulous!

Sara split the school neatly in half. Some thought the boys had it coming – they'd practically committed assault. Others thought she was using the situation. The papers were all over the place; the school was obviously a pit of sexual perversity and abuse, as if that sort of thing and worse had been going on for ages and no one had done anything about it. It was an object lesson in the way the press can make any old nonsense sound like truth.

Gradually, however, the hysteria died down; a consensus emerged. The boys were simply very immature. They needed to be taught a lesson, but a court case wasn't really it. Pressure built up on Sara. A number of people tried to get her to drop charges, including Teresa Dickinson, one of the original two girls who were friends with the boys.

'They were just mucking around, you know that,' she said.

'I turned a bunch of potential rapists into decent citizens, that's all I know,' replied Sara. 'No one gets to touch me unless I want them to – so tell that to your friends. And I've got plenty more where that came from.'

In the end, though, she did drop the charges. There was talk of expulsion, but the boys got away with a suspension for the rest of the term. Just as Sara said, they never did anything like that again. And they weren't the only ones. The school did actually have a problem – not quite as abusive as the press made out, but there was bullying going on. It was big against little, strong against weak, the tough against the delicate in that place, and had been for ages. The staff had turned a blind eye to a lot of it – some of them joined in – but now, with the world's eyes on them and their mistakes and failings reported in a suspicious press, they did something about it. They had no choice. Unfair she had been, maybe, but Sara put an end to a lot of tears and fears by her action.

That was her. Whatever she did, she did it full on and only started thinking about it afterwards.

As Sara grew older, she developed fabulous ambitions. Janet had no doubt that she would follow her star and that she could never go with her to such distant places. But although the two girls were developing in different directions, they somehow never grew apart. Right up to the end, they loved one another like sisters.

Sara had been taking lessons at the Stagecoach performance school for years, but by the age of twelve she was already saying that she was going to become famous for being herself rather than for any skills she might cultivate. At the same time, the question of exactly who she was became an issue. As a child, Sara had always enjoyed games of pretence, role plays, that sort of thing. But as she got older, instead of dropping them as most people do, she incorporated them more and more into her daily behaviour, to the point where it became difficult to separate what was real from what was make-believe.

It began with accents. She'd pick up an accent and speak it for days on end. She'd turn up on Monday morning in Irish, or Brummy or with a faint Japanese accent, and that was her for the week. But it was more than that; the voices developed lives of their own. They became new people. Often, they would have completely different tastes from Sara herself. Janet recalls characters who loved things Sara always hated, like red meat stewed in red wine, scraps with her fish and chips or T-shirts that hung down to her hips.

Janet found it bewildering. Sometimes she didn't like the new girls, but mostly she fell head over heels in love with them, just as she had with Sara herself. Then – pop! – she'd wake up one morning and they'd be gone. It used to spook her out.

Once, Sara was a Filipino girl for three weeks nonstop. Her name was Maria and she was twenty years old. She'd joined a marriage club back in the Philippines to find a Western husband and her parents had got her to marry an older man who'd brought her back to live in England. Now, she had to get a job and send back money and support the whole family, but she wanted to get some education first. Her husband was forty-five years old, and because he was a big cheese in the civil service he was able to pull a few strings. That's how her passport said she was a fifteen-year-old

English girl who was entitled to a free education instead of a twenty-year-old Filipino girl who wasn't. Maria was having to pretend all the time that she was English. She swore Janet to secrecy. She was prepared to do anything to get an education and look after her family. She said her husband was really kinky, hinting mysteriously at any number of weird sexual things she had to do without ever specifying them. She told Janet and her other friends that they were never to go with an older man because they were all pervs. But they all thought, because Maria was so innocent, it was probably something actually really rather normal, but no one ever liked to ask.

Maria stayed for three weeks and then disappeared, like all the others before and after her. Janet was mortified. She swore that while she was being Maria, Sara actually started to look Filipino.

'She had Filipino eyes, I swear it,' said Janet. 'It killed me. I really missed her. I couldn't believe I was so upset but that's how I felt. I made her do Maria one more time so she could say goodbye to me – I couldn't bear it that she'd just gone. We even worked out a happy ending for her, where she left her husband and found a lovely Filipino boy who took her away to live in America and really respected her.'

As well as becoming other people, Sara, at the age of fourteen, began to have visions. Ghosts, apparitions, voices. She never said much about that, even to Janet, and Janet was never sure how real they were, either. Sara once claimed that she had seen Maria walking around her bedroom packing up her clothes.

'Freaky!' said Janet. 'What was that about? Seeing your own inventions as ghosts after you've just killed them off!'

There are one or two other characteristics of Sara's that must be mentioned here, since they have an important bearing on what happened later on. One is Sara's reputed anorexia. Anorexia is a word much bandied about these days, in an age where thinness and beauty are more or less the same thing. Sara was never a lollipop-girl, never in any danger of starving herself to death, but was permanently on a diet she was never able to stick to – in short, she felt fat and ugly. The briefest glance at any photograph would tell anyone else that none of this was true.

And another thing: Sara had accidents. That would come as a surprise to many people who knew her, since she had tremendous grace and precision in her movements. People describe her as moving like a dancer just when making a cup of tea or leaning across to listen to someone speak. But she had accidents – not with things, but with herself. She spilt hot drinks down her front on several occasions, and had to be treated for burns. By the time she was seventeen, she had broken her arms and legs no less than four times, each time by falling down the stairs. Another time, she dropped a brick on her foot the day before she was due to enter the final of a dance competition, and spent the next two months in a cast, hobbling around on crutches.

These accidents have come under much suspicion. The suggestion is that Sara engineered them herself, in other words, that she self-harmed. It is a charge that she always denied, but, as many people have pointed out, Sara saying that something was true or false doesn't always mean much at all.

It was one such accident, just after she split up from Mark, that took her into the hospital where she first met Jonathon Heat.

A Brief History
of Jonathon Heat

Jonathon Heat is a man whose fame has many roots – as a multi-platinum-selling pop idol, as a creative artist, an art collector, a billionaire charity worker, as a human chameleon, fashion victim and, finally, as a heartless criminal, one of the monsters of our time. He has taken on so many forms, some beautiful, some bizarre, as his early good looks succumbed under endless rounds of surgery to a series of increasingly mask-like and beastly faces. But none of the many images we've had of him has been as striking as the recent ones from inside Strangeways Prison, taken when fellow inmates tore his protective mask off – the bared, mirthless grin of the death's-head, the bleeding skull, the terrifying spectacle of a man with no face.

The phenomenal global success of his early music – 'The Heat is On', 'Burning Heat', 'Endure the Heat' and so on – was followed by a lull that looked like the end of his career. At that point, Heat might have been no different from a handful of unusually successful chart-toppers. But within a year he returned with a dramatic reinvention of his music, his image and himself. The boy-band jeans and T-shirt were swapped for a skin-tight black suit and bootlace tie; the round, wistful face and blue eyes exchanged for a long chin, an arched nose and patchy black stubble. Most remarkably, gone were the chubby legs and meaty bum, replaced by long, razor-thin shins and an electric dance style that seemed to turn him into rubber. Heat's ability to reinvent himself encompassed not only his clothes, but his looks; not only his songs, but his voice; not only the way he moved, but even, apparently, his physical shape.

And the new look was not just skin deep: Heat changed his life along with his image. The following years saw a series of transformations that were personal as well as theatrical – his lifestyle, his relationships and even his sexuality changed over and over again, until change itself became his image. His second form was even more successful than the first; the third almost as successful as the second. After that, however, Heat's success began to wane. His older fans preferred the music they had first fallen in love with, his new morphs attracted fewer and fewer listeners. Newer styles and younger faces overtook him. Heat's star had made him as fabulous as a unicorn, as famous as Christ, but finally, at the age of thirty-one, even he was becoming a thing of the past.

Heat turned his attention to other things – his art collection, his own experiments in film and graphics, his charity work abroad and at home. For a few years, he hardly appeared as a performer at all. But the surgery that had been the cornerstone of his transformations continued. At this point, most of the procedures Heat had done were performed in London's Warehouse Clinic, and for a long time he seemed perfectly happy with the service they offered – fiddling with his nose and chin, sculpting his cheeks and forehead, tucking in his creases and lifting the flab – the usual sort of thing.

Things changed in his early thirties, when an outbreak of flu badly affected the staff at the Warehouse and, for a short period, they employed the services of the controversial surgeon Dr Wayland Kaye.

In his thirties and forties, Kaye had been a rapidly rising star in the field of cosmetic surgery, pioneering new techniques and doing research into tissue transplants across blood types, across body types, even, in the end, across species. For a while he had been a fashionable target for funding from all directions, but as his theories grew more and more outlandish and his claims increasingly extravagant, the money for research began to dry up. Kaye, by all accounts, felt betrayed and reacted badly; there were a number of very ugly scenes, some of them in public. As time passed, Kaye became increasingly willing to put even his more bizarre ideas into practice without the data or research to back them up – and, it was hinted, without the necessary legislation allowing him to go ahead. Prosecutions were in the pipeline, but nothing was ever proved. But his skill remained unquestioned, which is why, after a suitable period, clinics still occasionally brought him in for emergencies.

Kaye's ideas were wide-ranging, from simple surgical techniques for flesh sculpture, to drugs that would promote healing, prevent scarring and even apparently help flesh grow into the desired shape. They included the use of artificial skin, skin grown from other species and finally to that holy grail of cosmetic surgery, the full face transplant. It was, by all accounts, Dr Kaye's ambition to be the first man to carry one out successfully.

Heat and Kaye immediately recognised each other. Each had what the other wanted – Heat, fabulous amounts of money, a fascination with his own appearance and a willingness to experiment on his own person endlessly, while Kaye had the skills to perform the surgery and the vision of how things were going to be when the future came.

In 1998, Kaye set up his own private clinic with funds provided by Heat, who became the subject – some might say the victim – of many of Kaye's early experiments. And it has to be said that at first they were astonishingly successful. Kaye began by trying to reverse some of the problems with Heat's previous surgery – scarring, muscle tone and so on – as well as removing many of the natural effects of age. The result a few months later was that Heat seemed to have lost twenty years. If there was a problem it was not that his face looked overworked; it was that it looked too young for the rest of him.

Heat now relaunched his career as a performer – in a small way at first. But his plans were bigger than ever.

As his confidence in Kaye grew, so did Heat's ambition. He believed that Kaye was at the beginning of a revolution in facial surgery. People would soon be able to design faces for themselves almost as easily as they wore clothes. Mistakes would be rectified easily with no damage done.

Kaye, it appears, encouraged him in this belief. In 2000, Heat built a surgery into the basement of his house in Cheshire, where he and Dr Kaye began a series of startling experiments that caused shock waves around the world.

The first introduction to the world of Kaye's new techniques, and Heat's commitment to them, came with the release of Heat's 2001 album, *The Mark of the Beast,* in which Heat appeared at first on video, then on stage with his face stretched out into a beastly snout, a doggish look, complete with hair and canines. His appearance on *The Johnathan Ross Show,* caused a sensation when Ross jumped up in the middle of the interview and tried to pull off Heat's doggish facial hair, with the result that it proved to be completely real. Heat compounded the moment by jumping forward and snapping at Ross's hand; the clash of his hard white teeth was heard right around the world.

Heat maintained the illusion that his dog-face was real for years, but the reality was amazing enough. The dog hair on the sides of his face and chin was for real, as Ross had inadvertently revealed. Amazingly, so was the snout – but it was not a part of Heat. That is to say, not a permanent part. Kaye had removed the snout of a half-breed terrier and kept it alive with an artificial blood flow, until it was transplanted onto the front of Heat's face. No one could see the star's real mouth underneath it, and the nose, teeth and lips of the dog were obviously genuine. In fact, it was not a part of him at all, and clipped on round the back of the head, but no one knew that at the time. Dressed immaculately in a dark double-breasted pin-stripe, with a grey shirt and a big soft knot in his tie, Heat looked fabulously beastly. Women found it attractive; men copied it as best they could.

Heat gloried in it. Sales rocketed.

A number of other changes took place over the following years, in which Heat appeared as a cat and then as a demon, complete with horns and a forked tongue. No one was ever sure exactly how much trickery was involved, but a lot of the trickery itself was surgical. Kaye had taken surgery to places it had never been before. Looking young or beautiful or even normal was no longer the aim.

And yet... As far back as 2002, there were rumours of things going wrong. The rumours reached a crescendo in the year 2003. Heat responded with a move that utterly confounded his critics by suddenly appearing as himself, looking exactly as you might expect his thirty-nine-year-old self to look, if only he had not been through so much surgery. For a while it really did seem that it was now possible, using Kaye's techniques, to appear and reappear in the flesh, in whatever guise you wanted.

Heat went on tour again and released a new album, As I Am. Looking back, we can see blemishes on Heat's skin as far back as his first chat-show appearances to publicise the new tour and album. Stills taken during the tour illustrate the progress of the disintegration. In New York, there was heavy make-up on his face that close-ups reveal covered sticking plasters. In Los Angeles, hardly an inch of skin was showing under the make-up. In Moscow, his hairline slipped and it was obvious he was wearing a wig.

In Sydney, he was wearing a half-mask. In Hong Kong, it was a full mask. By this time, the entire structure of his face had collapsed. The tour was abandoned before he even reached Europe.

Under the mask, the wreckage was terrible. The skin had peeled off, the blood supply dried up, the nervous system gone haywire. Flesh had begun to die and to grow and to bleed without order. The muscles detached themselves from the bone and cartilage and sagged inside his skin -'like a bag of butcher's meat', as one ex-staff member put it. Masses of scar tissue began to form at an accelerated rate and, within a few months, Heat began to look more like the elephant man than an international idol.

Medical photographs leaked recently show Heat's face in various stages of disintegration. They reveal a shocking record of science gone horribly wrong. The effect on Heat, a man who was used to personal beauty, a vain man, someone who had relied on his looks all his life, was devastating. He entered a deep depression, was suicidal and at times apparently psychotic. He tried at least four times to kill himself and on several occasions attacked those around him. It has been suggested that if it were not for his huge wealth and the power that goes with it he would long ago have been confined to a mental institution. As always, he survived; but not as he was. That was nothing new for Heat, who had changed himself so many times. But, this time, the change was more than he had bargained for.

Kaye's experiments had finally gone wrong as his critics had always claimed they would, but Heat had nowhere else to turn. He clung on to the hope that the old man – Kaye was over eighty by this time – could still pull off another miracle. He poured money into new experiments, growing skin and flesh in culture, transplanting the faces of dogs, pigs and monkeys from one to the other, even, it's rumoured, from species to species, in an attempt to find a way of fixing what had gone wrong. Rumours abounded. There was something gothic and monstrous about this partnership – on the one hand Heat, who had taken beauty so far and at last destroyed it, and on the other the old man who had brought him to it, searching with his knife in the flesh of so many creatures, cutting and slicing, throwing away life after life down there under the mansion, in his attempts to undo his own work. Ambition and faith had taken both men to this; the first they could never surrender and the latter they did not dare to let go.

Kaye proclaimed himself confident of success. His aim, apparently and astonishingly, was actually to grow a new face for his protégé. That was some years off, and, in the meantime, he was in contact with hospitals all over the world. He still nurtured his ambition to perform the first full-face transplant in history, but to find one that matched Heat's genetic make-up wasn't going to be easy.

The world was certain that at last Heat's fabulous career was at an end. It's a measure of the man that from the ashes of his destruction, Heat managed not only to salvage something, but to create one of his most successful incarnations.

Heat was nearly forty when he launched the now famous Night of the Mask Tour. Every paying customer got a free mask as they entered the stadia and concert halls. Heat later described the sensation of seeing sixty thousand people all wearing the same face – his – as a terrifying but formative experience.

Over and over again, he had the cameras trained on the audience so they could see themselves while he made his famous statement: 'In real life, you are the performers and I am the audience.'

Dressing in the same way as Heat did had been a habit of his fans, both male and female, for years. The next day, the newspapers were full of the arresting image of all those people looking exactly the same as the man on stage – the same thin black trousers and short jacket, the same diagonally striped red-and-white T-shirt, and now, finally, the same face. It was everyone's opportunity to become Heat himself, for a night at least.

The records outsold anything he had done before, and the mask caught on everywhere he went. Of course, at this point, no one had any idea just how terrible the damage under the artificial face really was. The masks sold in their millions all around the world – some costing just a few pounds, some hundreds, but all looking the same. They were deliberately devoid of emotion or expression and were, as one newspaper suggested, a kind of living death mask. It's estimated that Heat made several million pounds from mask sales alone.

As that first tour began with a series of gigs in Heat's home town of Manchester, a few miles away, a teenage schoolgirl was looking in amazement at the rows of faces looking out at her from the newspapers. What made the whole experience so remarkable for Sara was that the mask so closely resembled her own face. For a while at least, she thought that Heat rmight have based the look directly on her. It was only later, when she saw earlier photos of him, that she realised he had based the face on an idealised version of what he had looked like years before. The fact was, she and the young Heat were so similar, they might have been twins.

Sara bought herself a mask that same day and began wearing it as often as she could get away with it. She dyed her blonde hair black and wore it in the loose ringlets Heat wore. She wore his clothes and imitated his walk and his accent. Like millions of other boys and girls the world over, she did everything she could to become Jonathon Heat. But, like all fashions, this new version of Jonathon Heat had its shelf life. The sales of masks declined; the third album, *Who We Is*, didn't sell well. For the fourth or fifth time in his career, Heat was yesterday's man. But for Sara the fascination with him had only just begun.

Over the years there had been a good deal of 'behaviour' from Sara, as her mother referred to it. A lot of it was normal enough – tantrums, shouting and swearing, breaking things around the house – stuff not uncommon in people her age. But there were other things that might have indicated that Sara's sense of identity was becoming shaky. At the time, they seemed bizarre, but not bizarre enough to indicate actual illness – more like exaggerated personality traits. Her use of accents is one example. The way she used masks is another.

Sara had always been fond of masks. When she found one she liked, she would often wear it for days. Included in the list of masks she had worn as a girl were a witch mask from Halloween, a Guy Fawkes mask from 5th November, a Cherie Blair mask she had once kept on for two whole days, even in her sleep, and a number of animal masks she had had when she was little. When she got old enough to use make-up, she liked to apply it thickly, even though it wasn't the fashion. In the years prior to the Heat mask, she developed a habit of doing self-portraits that bore little or no resemblance to herself. These portraits did not have any set of features that stuck. There might be a period of a few months when they all looked like the same person, but then they'd change, overnight. The pattern was repeated many times with other faces.

Sara's mother, Jessica, wasn't particularly bothered by the mask at first. Sara wore the mask when she was out, but at home she rarely bothered with it. Sometimes she'd put it on when a friend came round – but then quite often the friend was wearing one as well. It was weird, but no weirder to her mother's eyes than a lot of things girls do at that age – no weirder than a lot of things she used to do herself.

But from school a different story began to emerge. Heat masks had been tolerated in the playground and at breaks but soon mask-wearing began to spread beyond Heat fans into the general population. There was a suspicion that they were being used by gangs to hide their identities when committing crimes. Newspapers began to carry shock stories; the street fashion of wearing hoodies over the mask began to spread to school; the school became alarmed and the masks were banned.

There were some complaints. A few students tried to sneak them in, but it was all dealt with fairly easily – except for Sara. She seemed completely unable to comply with this simple instruction.

Her teachers were alerted at once – it wasn't like her at all. Ellen Simpson, her art teacher, said she hardly recognised her when she tried to get her to take it off.

'She just said no. Then, when I insisted, she almost threw a fit,' she recalled. Sara was normally a well-behaved girl – talkative and often overexcited, but thoughtful and keen to do well. She loved imagery of all kinds and could get very excited over artwork, and she had a good relationship with her teacher. Now, suddenly, her behaviour was so disruptive that Ellen had to take her out into the corridor to try to calm her down.

'It was hopeless,' she said. 'Eventually she just stormed off. I had to report her to her head of year.'

Things went from bad to worse, with neither Sara nor the school prepared to back down. For the first time in her life, Sara was missing lessons. She tried to come back with her face bare and then put the mask on in school, hiding it with her arm during lessons – she obviously didn't want to miss school but simply could not bear to have her face exposed. At home, once the letters began to arrive and the problem was out in the open, Sara took to wearing the mask indoors all the time as well. Suddenly, she would not be seen without it. She wore it in bed. She wore it watching

TV or reading. She wore it when she was eating, lifting it up to tuck mouthfuls of food underneath. She even took to bathing and sleeping in it. It was round about this time that her mother heard her shouting abuse in her room. When she ran up to investigate, Sara was there alone and claimed she'd had the radio on loud, but eventually Jessica got to the bottom of it. Her daughter was shouting abuse at the mirror.

'The next time I crept upstairs to listen. "Who's that girl? Who's that girl? Get her out of here," she was shouting – at her own reflection! It made my hair stand on end.'

It was at this point that Jessica made an appointment with a psychiatrist. Sara was just fifteen years old. She was unable to go to school and spent most of her days mooching around the house in her mask on her own while her mother went to work. It was during this period that most of the accidents happened. Still, things got better fairly quickly. She was attending school again a few months later, although she was doing very little work and was being a great annoyance to her teachers. She'd missed a sizeable chunk of the GCSE course and obviously had no intention of catching up. As she said to one teacher, 'The only bits of paper I want in my hand are recording contracts.' As soon as she left school she got a part-time job and spent the rest of her time supposedly practising her dancing and singing – although in fact, according to her mother, she spent most of it lying in bed. By the time she met Mark, some eighteen months after she first got into trouble at school, she was hardly wearing the mask at all.

I've mentioned Sara's accidents before. There were several over the years, starting when she was twelve, when she spilt scalding tea down her front, reaching a crescendo during her obsessive mask-wearing and fading away in her sixteenth year. By the time she was seventeen, like the masks, the accidents seemed to be a thing of the past. Then came the most bizarre one of all.

Sara was ironing her clothes and somehow managed to get her feet entangled in the flex. She tripped and fell onto the ironing board, which twisted round under her weight. Sara somehow got her arms stuck in between the legs and the board, stopping her from protecting her face as she fell. She struck her head on the bookcase as she went down, temporarily stunning her. She landed face down with the hot iron pressed firmly against her left cheek.

How long she lay like that no one can tell, since she was on her own, but it was long enough to brand her face with an indelible mark, a red triangle rising from her jaw line and pointing to the middle of her brow. She came to with the smell of burning flesh in her nostrils. Her mother came rushing up the stairs to the sound of her screams and found her staring in the mirror, the iron in one hand, the board in a tangle on the floor and clothes everywhere.

'Don't worry,' exclaimed Sara, as her mother rushed to hold her. 'I can get it fixed at the same time as my nose.'

The accident, as Sara herself pointed out, was hardly credible. Certainly neither her mother nor her psychiatrist believed her story, although Sara insisted it was the bald truth right to the end.

The doctors calculated that the iron must have been pressed against her face for a good five seconds or more for the heat to have penetrated so deeply. There was much they could do with creams and other treatments, but, surgery apart, Sara was scarred for life.

As a result of this, Sara was sent to hospital for a few days, 'under observation'. Whether this was to watch her burns, or for fear that she might hurt herself more, the information protection act forbids us from finding out. It was there, in wards of the Manchester Royal Infirmary, despite objections from the nursing staff, that she started to wear her Heat mask again. And it was there, too, that Jonathon Heat came into her life. It was like a dream come true for Sara. We all have dreams; we all hope they'll come true for us, but they rarely do. For Sara, tragically, this one did.

Sara — 7 April 2005

(Sara is in a toilet, presumably in the hospital. She's propped her camera up and she's sitting on the toilet, speaking in an excited whisper. She's wearing a mask, covering her face down to her nose and both cheeks, hiding her face. The mask is one of those popularised by the rock star Jonathon Heat. Her eyes are as bright as jewels shining through the mask.)

Imagine, right, you're lying in hospital and the sister comes in and says someone wants to see you, so you say who and she says...Jonathon Heat! Can you imagine that? Ridiculous. I mean, what? But you know he does this thing visiting hospitals and ill people, all that – that charitable stuff. But here – with me! Everyone else was saying they thought she was having us on, but I knew at once. I knew. I felt it right here, in between my ribs. That's where premonition hurts you, on this spot. You get a twinge there, a ghost, or something like it, is coming close. You think things. I was actually thinking it just a few minutes before; I was thinking, Here I am feeling completely miserable, I've really fucked up yet again, but wouldn't it be fantastic if some mega-rich superstar walked in to visit me and made all my dreams come true? It happens. It has to happen to someone; it can happen to me.

And now he was really coming! So the first part of my wish had already come true ...

I'm so excited. It's like having a – I don't know, a fairy godmother here in the ward with me. He's a genie, really; people that rich and famous, they're like genies, there's something magical about them. I was scared, because this is magic, real magic, the real thing. I know my dreams and ambitions can only come true through magic. I believe in magic. And I was scared because, like, maybe I'd suddenly got the power to make wishes come true. I was scared even to think that thought in case I wished for the wrong thing. Hey! Isn't that crazy? Like, you know ... sometimes I have bad thoughts inside me. Harmful things. I could hurt people if they ever got out.

But that's just nonsense. What's real is – this is real; this is my big chance. I ballsed up big time and let myself down. But out of it – well. Anything could come out of it. And I knew at once what I was going to do. I know it was cheeky. I am cheeky. I'm the cheekiest person on this whole planet, let me tell you! I know he's kind. He's famous for being kind. So I had to do it. I had to ask him to make my dreams come true. So I did.

When he came in, I mean actually walked into the ward, I was shocked. I'd seen him so many times on TV, it was like looking at someone who didn't even exist. Isn't that amazing, that you can get so famous that it's like you don't exist any more? Like you become fictional.

And all the time they have a real life. That doesn't make sense; I love things like that that are true and make no sense. They shit and wee and cough and sniff flowers and make tea. That's what fascinated me the most – what he was really going to be like, I mean, really like, without the cameras. Anyway, so he came in. He was a story walking into the ward. He came down between the beds, turning his head this way and that, saying something no one could hear to one of his aides. He looked so unreal, just like he does on film. I mean, he looks unreal in real life! Amazing. And he dresses up all the time, just like you see him on stage – he had on one of those black suits with a kind of frock coat, you know, quite long, and cowboy boots. But you couldn't see all of his face, because of course he had the mask on, the famous Jonathon Heat mask. He never takes it off. All you could see was his eyes and part of his mouth. They say his lips aren't real. Ugh. That mask, it was a top-quality one, though. Honest, it looked like real skin. When he came up close, when he was just a few feet away from me looking into my eyes, it looked really spooky, because it really does look like real skin. There was a mole on it. Wow. What if it is . . . ?

He came along, nodding and chatting to some of the patients, but I knew who he was after because he kept glancing over in *my* direction. Mine. Me, me, me. Heh, heh, heh. All the time he was talking to the other people he was looking at me. He winked at me. See? Oh, he was mine!

He went along from person to person with the sister and then at last he arrived at my bed.

'This is Sara,' said the sister.

And Jonathon smiled and said, 'Sara, I know.' My hand went up to my face; I thought he must be referring to that, to my burns. I had a mask on. But he shook his head. 'No, no. Not that, not your face. You. I recognise you.'

Wow! I peered up at him to see if he was joking, but he wasn't. I thought, Does he mean it? Is he just being weird – because, let's face it, when you get that famous you're weird already, by default. No one's ever going to treat you like a human being ever again. Or was he just sucking up – you know how people do with sick people. They tell you how special you are. But they don't mean special. They mean *special*.

'The other patients are over here...' the sister began, but Jonathon smiled at her and said, 'I'd like to stop here and talk to Sara for a while, if I may. I believe this young lady and I have a lot in common.'

Sister nodded. 'Let me know when you're ready,' she said briskly, and walked off, as if wanting to talk to me was some kind of crime.

I was just staring at him, trying to soak in that this was a real, living human being who just happened to be more famous than anyone else who had ever been alive, practically. Do you think, if you get so famous that so many people are thinking about you at any one time, and so many people love you and idolise you, that you can become like someone people pray to? Like, they carry so much human attention

41

around with them, they could point it at you and make things happen if they felt like it? You know what I mean? That they can...I don't know, bless you or something, just by being near you. That was how it felt with him. And here he was, standing next to my bed, looking down at me like I was a bag of his favourite sweets.

His aides moved off a little bit to give us some privacy and he sat down on the edge of the bed. Jonathon Heat sitting on the side of your bed. Wow! My mum would have paid in flesh for that to happen to her. I was watching him, trying to read him – you know, was he just being nice, or was he trying to chat me up or did we really, really have a special bond? I was just biting the sides of my cheeks to stop myself from grinning like an idiot.

'You're wearing one of my masks,' he said, frowning a little bit. 'But a girl like you doesn't need to hide her face.'

'Oh, I like wearing it,' I told him, and my blood ran cold because I knew he was going to want to see my face and... I'd had that accident, you see. I didn't want him to see my burns. I mean, actually, I don't say this to my mum or any of the shrinky people, because they'd take it all wrong – but I'm proud of my burns. I don't want to be pretty. I want to be so much more than pretty!

But he didn't know that about me yet. I blushed at the thought of it. Of course he'd know about the burns. They'd have told him all about me. He'd think that I was some sort of psycho. But, anyway, he changed the subject.

'I hear you're a very talented girl; everyone here tells me that.'

'Oh, I practise a little. Nothing like you, Mr Heat,' I said, although, actually, Heat doesn't have the best voice in the world. It's being famous he's good at.

'I know you sing, Sara. I hear you have a lovely voice. Do you know "Allie's Song"?'

I wasn't even going to have to ask him. He was doing it all for me!

'Allie, do you know,' I warbled, all nervous. I must have sounded dreadful, I was so scared, my throat was tight. He smiled at me and we sang it together while everyone in the whole ward listened.

> 'Allie, do you know where your heart is?
> Do you even know where your home is now?
> Did you give it all away,
> Did you leave it all behind,
> Did you forget what it meant to you and me?
> Come home, come home, love,
> Come home with me.
> But, she said, I don't need a home.
> I'll drink your love instead.
> But she said, she said,
> I don't need a heart.
> I'll just be yours instead.'

It was so beautiful. I say it myself, but it's true. Our voices really worked together. Everyone, even the aides, they all turned round to listen and when it was over they clapped us. It was a dream, but it was real.

'Sara, that was wonderful. You really are very talented.'

And some of the aides standing nearby who'd heard, I could see them nodding and agreeing with him, so I knew it wasn't just him putting it on.

'Is it true you want to be a singer?'

All I could do was nod, I was so choked up. I couldn't believe what was happening!

'You're going to go a long way with that voice,' he told me.

We talked for ages. Don't ask me about what, I can't remember most of it. People said after that he sat with me for ages, but I lost all track of time. We talked about all sorts. About each other's families, about his career, all that sort of thing. And, at the end, he did something special. Very personal. Something that I'm never going to tell anyone. But I'll tell you, anyway, because this diary is for my eyes only.

'Sara,' he said. 'I want to ask you something. I know what a big thing it is to ask, because people ask me from time to time as well and it always makes me feel awful, so I'd only ask it for a very special reason.'

'What is it?' I said, and my heart began to beat so hard, it hurt. And the other strange thing, I had a pain here; the place for premonitions. But there was no ghost. Now, what does that mean?

'Sara,' he said quietly, leaning in to speak softly to me. 'Sara, show me your face.'

I couldn't say no. I just couldn't say no. All down one side was red and ugly. He was going to get me to show him how ugly I was, but I couldn't say no to him. And it was right, too, I knew that. Because, to achieve that sort of fame, you have to be prepared to show everything. I felt my hand going up to the mask, but before it got there he put his hand on mine and said, 'Wait.'

Then he did it. He stared straight into my eyes and lifted his mask. He lifted up his mask like he never did, not for anyone, and he showed me his face.

It was awful. Awful, awful, awful! You know those pictures of him when he was young, how lovely he was? And now he was awful. The skin was hanging off, there were bits of it stuck on almost like they'd been glued. I found out later they were grafts, some of it was red raw, some of it was stretched and shiny like it had been burned and healed into loads of scars. With the mask on he looked gorgeous; but underneath – underneath he was a monster. I'd never seen anything like it.

'You see me as I am, Sara,' he said, looking straight into my eyes. 'And I did this to myself. Too many operations, too much surgery. At the time I thought I was helping myself, but now I realise that was just an excuse I was hiding behind. I was hurting myself, Sara. I was making myself look ugly because I felt ugly inside. The whole world thought I was beautiful, but I felt ugly. That's my illness: ugliness. I was more afraid of being ugly than anything in the world, and now I've made myself exactly that.'

He paused for a bit to let it sink in, still staring at me. I was half aware of the ward sister having a conversation with his aides and trying to get past – like he was doing something wrong! – but the aides were getting in her way until he'd finished.

He put his mask back on. 'Sara, I believe we're kindred spirits, you and me,' he told me. 'We both love singing and dancing and entertaining people and making them happy. We both want to challenge how people think of themselves. We both want to bring good to the world. We're both talented, we're both beautiful, but inside, Sara...Do you think maybe you could be like me? Do we both have some devil who keeps telling us how ugly we are, and sometimes, when we're feeling weak, we're stupid enough to believe it? Do you understand what I'm saying?'

I knew what he meant. He meant that I had hurt myself – that I had put the iron to my face. All I could do was nod. He was describing himself, but he wanted me to be like him and I couldn't deny him, could I? I couldn't say he wasn't like me, even if it was true.

'Sara, show me your face.' It was a command. I took off my mask.

He looked at me for a long time. Then he beckoned with a finger to one of his aides, who came over. It was an old guy, he must have been over eighty. Later, I found out it was Dr Kaye. He bent down and examined the burned skin, asked me a few questions.

At last he nodded. 'It's not serious. We can fix that.'

Jonathon smiled. He looked happy. 'I was hoping I wasn't too late,' he said. And, honestly, you know what? There were real tears in his eyes. 'You're a beautiful girl, Sara. I want to help you. I don't want you to become a monster like me.'

'You're not a monster,' I squeaked. But he shook his head.

'It's possible to turn yourself into a monster, Sara. I'm the living proof of it. I want to help. But first, Sara, I want you to make me a promise.'

He reached out and laid his hand gently on my cheek.

'This is my face,' he said, stroking me. 'When you harm it, you harm me. And these are my hands,' he said, stroking my hand, which I had lifted up to lay on his. 'When they harm you, I am harming you.'

'It was an accident,' I said.

'OK,' he said. 'Accident on purpose?' He smiled at me but I didn't answer or even shake my head. I felt that the demon in me was already half healed, but more awake than ever.

'I promise,' I said. And I knew I'd keep my word.

What she didn't know then was what it was she'd really promised.

Home Manor Farm

Within the month, Sara had gone to live at Heat's Cheshire mansion, Home Manor Farm.

It was all done properly. She was seventeen and regarded herself as her own master, but Heat insisted on getting her mother's permission. Jessica was all for it. Heat wanted to get her father in on it as well, but Jessica was having none of it.

'Once Tony found out, he'd've never let go,' she said. She was talking about money. Tony Carter was a moderately successful businessman, running a small factory in Wiltshire packaging biscuits and other snacks for the hotel industry. Whether he would have been as predatory as Jessica claimed, we'll never know, as Heat respected her wishes and kept him very much at arm's length. A minor figure in all this, Tony Carter's only significance in Sara's life is his absence. Heat has used his own brief attempt to get him involved as evidence against the accusation that Sara was kept as isolated as possible at Home Manor Farm while he carried out his crimes.

Jessica herself was involved, but apart from a short period at the beginning, not at the house. Heat gave her a job that kept her away from her daughter as much as possible, but, in his favour, there is universal agreement that Sara and Jessica together in Heat's house was not a good idea. Sara obviously didn't want her mother around and Jessica herself was overexcited and anxious about the whole thing. She may have been jealous, or alarmed. She never felt in control of Sara, and their lives together had been punctured with furious rows for years. She was by all accounts a confirmed flake, with a strong tendency to create a crisis and then go to pieces in it.

'She'd just have made things worse,' said Janet. 'She was always getting in the way. And if Sara did want her she'd just get cross. They loved one another, I suppose, but they didn't get on terribly well. I just don't think she understood Sara at all.'

Which isn't terribly surprising since no one else does, either.

It's certainly true that Jessica had very little respect for the things that Janet herself valued her friend for – her incredible imagination and flights of fancy.

'She told lies about everything from a very early age,' Jessica told *Wow!* magazine later on. 'Who broke this jug? It was the cat, Mummy. Who's been in my make-up bag? A little girl came to the door and said she had something for you so I let her upstairs; it must have been her, Mummy. She'd tell you something absolutely ridiculous and be mortally offended if you didn't take her seriously. Who smashed my bedroom mirror, who tore up my nightie?

'It wasn't me, Mummy. it wasn't me. it was the gnomes who live under the bed. They said they'd behave and I believed them!'

The tension between mother and daughter was tangible. Heat sent Jessica off to do location work with a film project he was developing. She spent most of the next weeks travelling around the world to exotic destinations, staying in nice hotels and being paid a lot of money for doing it. Despite her complaints about being separated from her daughter, Jessica seemed very happy with the arrangement at the time.

Even before Sara moved in, Heat was making plans for her future. Of course there would be records – a single, an album, and a video to go with it. There would be photo shoots. The fashion photographer Tiffany Gray was brought in within days to take the first shots. There would be dance lessons, singing lessons, every sort of lesson – some of them with Heat himself.

And there would be surgery. Heat wanted her face fixed as soon as possible.

Surprisingly, Sara was not so keen on this. Although she had been terribly upset when she had burned her face, she had almost come to like it. The burn was healing quickly and leaving behind a neat triangular patch of tight red skin, which she rapidly integrated as a part of her appearance. She sometimes painted another matching triangle on the other side and later, as the skin healed, she coloured the scar or decorated it in other ways.

'It's kinda African, don't you think? Sort of punk,' she told Heat, who apparently had to turn away, he was so upset, even though he had made a similar sort of aesthetic popular himself. Things had changed. A man whose face had been utterly destroyed, he couldn't bear the thought that someone with such good looks was prepared to miss a chance to restore herself, Sara, paradoxically, remained very keen on having her breasts re-sculpted, work done on her nose and cheek-bones, which she regarded as not well-defined enough, as well as something done about the fat on her thighs. But she wasn't at all sure about getting the scar fixed. Heat argued she might as well get her scar sorted while the rest of it was done. He got so agitated she agreed after various members of his staff intervened on his behalf.

'She was just winding him up if you ask me,' one of them said later on.

'It was the least she could do,' added someone else. Heat's generosity was legendary, and in return his staff were famous for their loyalty. By and large, the least you could do was anything possible.

Sara was a striking-looking girl, but not everyone would call her beautiful – there was something mask-like about her features which gave her an odd look that some saw as surreal, others angelic, and some merely bland. Seen without her make-up, her features were elfin and dainty, her skin very smooth and fine, with a neat nose, and a bright, lippy smile, disconcertingly wide, which changed her entire face when she turned it on. She had striking green eyes, very large and liquid with unusually large irises. It was the one feature that came across on film when she was wearing her mask.

Tiffany Gray took a number of sets of Sara, some with, some without her mask, and was very satisfied with the results.

Sara insisted they try to use her scar.

'She even said she might get it done again if Heat made her have it removed,' said Tiffany, shaking her head partly in wonder and partly in amusement. 'Sara had some very radical ideas about personal beauty. She thought if Jonathon could get to look like a dog, why couldn't she have her scar?'

But the thing that attracted Gray about Sara was that her look was so versatile – a different pose or the right lighting could change her whole appearance. The sets Gray took showed Sara seductive, cold, aggressive, passive and sexy in turn. In none of them do you get a sense of her as a person, but as Gray said, 'What do you expect? I was doing fashion, not a portrait.'

It's one of these images that developed cult status among students for a while, of Sara, wearing a white vest, naked from the waist down in heavy shadow with her face and the upper parts of her body emerging into a bright, warm light, staring down at the camera. Despite her assertive stance, there is something vulnerable about her. The huge eyes shining brightly from behind that bland plastic face seem to have possessed her.

Gray had been covering Heat for ages, but by this time she already considered him to be a predator who never did anything unless there was something in it for him. Privately, she advised Sara to have nothing more to do with him. Sara, she said, stared at her as if she was some sort of animal when she offered this piece of advice.

'Which I guess is only natural,' shrugged Gray. 'Heat must have looked like a dream ticket to her, but with her looks, she could have made it onto every catwalk in the world.'

Kaye did not want to operate until Sara's scars had healed properly, and planned on working on her sometime in July, a couple of months after she moved in. Decisions were being made very early on about the proposed changes to her breasts, her nose, her mouth, her cheeks and her thighs. Looking at the list, it seems extraordinary that a girl of only seventeen, with such looks as Sara had, should ever consider having so much work done. Janet, we know, was extremely concerned about it, but Sara was, as she described it later on, 'just delighted that she had that chance.' Gray, who had admired her so much at the photoshoot, never knew about the surgery; Sara never said a word. If she had known, 'I would have kicked her arse so hard she'd have needed surgery to put that right for her.' In Gray's opinion, it may have been the very simplicity that made her so versatile that Sara didn't like about her appearance.

'She just wanted everything about her to be extraordinary,' she said. 'Maybe she never realised that to be extraordinary to the camera isn't the same as looking extraordinary in real life.'

Sara's mother, who might have been expected to have intervened, found the whole idea of surgery so off-putting that she simply washed her hands of it.

'You decide. I don't want to even have to think about it,' she told Sara. And Sara took her at her word.

Heat's motives for wanting her to have surgery have been endlessly argued over. Despite, or perhaps because of, what had happened to him, he seemed to regard it all as very ordinary, but he was aware of Sara's youth and vulnerability on some level. Heat is on record as saying that he was totally unprepared for his own journey from schoolboy to star, and it's possible that he was more worried about Sara on that account. In fact, there is some evidence that he regarded the surgery as part of her preparation for that journey itself. For whatever reason, he insisted that his young protégé attend counselling sessions three times a week. Which, on the surface, sounds like a very good thing. Except that he chose Kaye to counsel her – the very man who had destroyed his own face.

Bernadette McNalty, a trained nurse who had been with Heat for years and who actually had more counselling training than Kaye anyway, was on the premises at the time. She would have been further removed from the operation and better placed to spot anything amiss. The Heat camp have pointed out that Bernadette was leaving to do some charity work in Jamaica the week after Sara moved in. Others have suggested that the choice of Dr Kaye was more simple – to ensure that Sara went ahead with procedures that Heat wanted.

The nature of Sara's relationship with Kaye is something we know very little about. According to Janet, Sara took against him right from the start. 'Dr Ghoul the face-eater,' she called him, and used to make jokes that he'd stolen Heat's face and swallowed it whole, like a jellyfish, while he was under anaesthetic. Janet told me that Sara spent her sessions with Kaye mucking around, making up voices and personalities. 'She told me she did a different person every other day, almost,' she said. Heat, to whom Kaye had to report, has never denied this, but puts a very different slant on it. According to him, Kaye and Sara explored various issues through role play, which accounts for the different voices. Kaye, he says, reported that the sessions were a great deal of fun but also very useful; they covered a lot of ground using aliases and different voices that they might not otherwise have touched on. It was how Sara preferred to deal with issues. Kaye looked forward to the sessions, and as far as Heat was concerned, so did Sara. This has been confirmed by various members of the Heat household.

Each session was filmed and recorded, and Kaye wrote up detailed reports on Sara's progress; but all records, including the ones Kaye kept on Heat, were destroyed in the fire that burned Home Manor Farm to ashes a few days after Sara left. Nothing was recovered. The nature of Sara's relationship with the mysterious Wayland Kaye remains unknown to us.

The troubles that came later must have seemed very distant to Sara when she first moved in. She was in heaven. Heat was working with her, already planning her first CD; within days they were already choosing songs and musicians to work with and they had already found a designer to coordinate her look. And in a few weeks' time, there was to be a party at which Sara and Heat were to recreate the opening number of the famous Night of the Mask Tour, in front of a galaxy of A-list celebrities, producers and entertainment promoters. It was to be her big launch.

And there were endless shopping trips, and eating out, and meeting other stars. Sara loved it. She was having the time of her life.

Sara – 5 May 2005

(Sara is walking around holding her camera and filming as she walks. She sounds as if she can't believe what's happening to her.)

This is my bedroom. Look at that! That's a sofa. It's about as long as my old room in Levenshulme. You could go to sea in it. You could fit my whole house in here. Table and chairs in the window. TV the size of Lithuania. It's like a showroom. Here's the view out of the window. Cherry trees in five different colours! They're not all out yet. And there's bits of his modern art collection in between the trees. There. Some of it looks like rubbish. Some of it *is* rubbish. Some of it looks like giant sloth turds left here twenty thousand years ago, but it's art. Ha ha! He gets people to pour blue dye down those pipes into the soil to the roots, it turns the flowers blue. Now, you have to admit, that's pretty cool! I can't wait. Blue cherries! I wonder if he gets blue cherries? I'll have to ask him about that.

Bathroom. Huge. Dressing room! He keeps taking me shopping. I need a whole separate room to keep my clothes in now. And *that's my* bed. Did you ever see anything like that? See, I couldn't get to sleep in this room, it's so huge. It was like trying to sleep on a football pitch. I like to be able to snuggle down, you know what I mean? So I asked Jonathon for a small room but he couldn't bear that – me, his guest of honour, in a little bitsy room – so he got me this giant bed instead, because it's as big as a small room. You can live in it. You can pull the curtains like this, so it can be all private whenever you like. This is the TV screen, it folds away into the wall like this, how cute is that? This is where you keep your books and CDs and things. This is a PlayStation. I keep clothes and stuff in this cupboard. Here's the stereo and headphones and all that. This is the fridge! A bed with an on-board fridge! Yes, yes, yes! Oh so dangerous, though. Everlasting snacks. He thinks I don't eat enough. He's part of the international conspiracy to make me fat. It's fun though and, even better, it's expensive fun. Yes. It gives me a lot of pleasure having all this money spent on me. That strange black-and-green gob going up one of the posts is more art. Jonathon did it. Jonathon can't tell the difference between art and ridiculous, so there's more ridiculous than art. But, if you ask me, this bed is so ridiculous, it's turned into art despite itself.

Now I'm coming round the front so you can see me. The camera goes on that ledge there . . .

Like that.

You're very privileged to be allowed in here. I don't allow anyone in here except my best friends, not even Jonathon. After the bed was delivered he came in to have a look at it.

He had to try it out – well, you could understand that: as soon as you see it you want to bounce on it, or get in there and pull the curtains. But he pulled himself right in so he was lying across it, and he just stayed there, sort of eyeing me up. I got up and went to sit in a chair on the other side of the room, about four hundred metres away and we had to shout at each other across the yawning chasm between us.

So what about it? The question is – does he want to shag me? Maybe the bed is one enormous casting couch. And the other questions is – do I want to shag him? You know what? It may have to be done. It's the price you have to pay. These guys, you have to love them or the story never happens. Hey, he must be quite good at it by now, all the practice he's had, that's one thing. But another thing is, well, he's so old! He's like yer granddad on a fashion shoot. How will I stop myself laughing when he gets going? Shagging granddads – I mean, yeeeew!

Maybe I don't mind. Shagging Jonathon Heat – why not? It'd be a pity not to, really.

On the other hand, it might be he's not like that at all. He's not very good at what stuff means. Behaviour, you know? He gets it all wrong. It might be him being all autistic. Maybe he really just wants to be my girlfriend and lie around on the bed reading *Heat* magazine and eating crisps and talking about diets and clothes and stuff.

Like hell. Anyway, I've got this great story about that. See, everyone always tells him exactly what he wants to hear, you know? The staff. It's like they've all convinced themselves that he's this wonderful person who can do no wrong, you know?

I mean, like, criticising Jonathon is just such bad manners. But the only one who doesn't go along with it is Bernadette. She's great. She's this Jamaican lady; she's been here for years. She used to help with the surgery and stuff but she started not to like it – well, she was right, wasn't she? But she and Jonathon were such good friends she stayed on to do other things. She's dead friendly; she's always popping in and out to see how things are going. She's quite quiet – she's one of those people who doesn't say much, but you always know exactly what they're thinking, you know what I mean?

Anyway, there was Jonathon stretched out on my bed, trying to make out what I was saying – I was being a bit mean, really. I was talking very quietly and I think he might be a bit deaf. Then there was this knock at the door, and I said, 'Come in,' dead quick, and in comes Bernadette. You should have seen Jonathon's face! It was obvious he knew he shouldn't be there. She was talking to me about stuff, but she was looking over at him the whole time and he was writhing about, trying to get off without her noticing. The bed's so huge you can't just slip off, especially if you've plonked yourself smack in the middle, so he had to sort of worm his way to the edge of it while she wasn't looking. It was so funny!

Finally she caught my eye and her eyebrows went up and we both suddenly smiled at each other – then that was it. I was cracking up. She had to pinch her lips together to stop herself smiling.

'Mr Heat,' she said. 'Do you think it's appropriate that you should be cavorting about on Sara's bed like that?'

'I wasn't cavorting, Bernadette,' he said. Cavorting! What sort of word is that? I can't imagine Jonathon cavorting. I didn't know where to look.

'Her mother's only just down the corridor, you know.'

He almost jumped off the bed when she mentioned Jessica, like she was lurking outside the door or something. I don't know why he should be scared of her. 'It's not like that, Bernadette,' he said.

And he was so embarrassed! You see, he really is sweet. He was writhing all around the floor almost, saying how sorry he was and everything, and how he didn't mean it like that and so on, and then he practically ran out of the room. You could see even under his mask that he'd gone bright red. His ears were blazing. They were sticking out of the side of that mask; they were so red they looked sore. He's so sweet!

'Poor Jonathon,' said Bernadette. And we both looked at each other and we both started snorting with laughter, but we couldn't laugh out loud in case Jonathon was still outside. She's great. It was hilarious! I had to go into the bathroom, I was making so much noise.

But she had to go away. Doing some charity stuff for Jonathon in Jamaica. Pity.

So listen: next week we're having a party. Jonathon is inviting forty people and I'm inviting forty people and we're going to perform together and – and guess what we're doing? The opening sequence from the Night of the Mask! The big one! Together. Me and Jonathon Heat. Think about that while you die of jealousy! It's going to be my big break. He'll have all the stars there and agents and film people – everyone. They'll see me. They'll see *me* . . .

He says I'm the best talent he's seen. For my age, I mean, and the fact that I've not had much proper training so far. He said, 'Sara, you know, I asked Georgie – ' (that's the voice coach) – 'what he thought of you and he said, "Platinum talent Jonathon – pure platinum."'

Platinum talent! That's me!

Only you can never entirely trust people with Jonathon, because, like I say, they all love him so much. In this house, even thinking Jonathon's a vain and stupid man is an act of purest evil. Yeah, and he pays them too and all . . .

But he is. Vain and stupid. It's just that he's also very, very sweet and he happens to be one of the most talented people on earth. Ha!

Meanwhile I'm getting myself really sorted out. His nutritionist is giving me loads of advice; I'm eating really healthily. Loads of fruit and stuff, lots of fish. Vegetables. I feel like a greengrocer. All organic. I'm getting loads of exercise. I'm feeling great! I swim, I work out, I have massages and saunas. Jonathon has a whole private health clinic here. My skin is glowing. I've had my hair done. Look at me: I look like something out of a magazine. If Mark could see me now – wow. Well, boy, you lost what you ain't never gonna get. The only problem is my weight – I can't seem to get rid of it. Look at this flab. Ugh! And here.

(She pinches a neat little fold of skin between her fingers.)

I look like the blubber bunny. And for the other stuff, the stuff you can't fiddle with, I've already got that booked in. The face – they're going to use a skin graft from my lily-white thighs. I don't care about that, that's for Jonathon. Like, it's my face anyway, what's up with him? But I guess if he wants to make me a big star he has to have a say in what I look like because that's all part of it.

The nose is going to be straightened. You can see. There. Like a bulbous – well, like a bulb. I wouldn't be surprised if it sprouted daffodils. I wanted them to suck out some of my lard, but they won't do that. They say I'm thin enough. So what's this, then? Is it bone? No. Is it muscle? No. It wobbles, therefore it's fat. Fat therefore I am.

You need to do that sort of thing in today's entertainment world. People say, What's the point if you have natural good looks, but that's not the point. The point is, this is art. It isn't natural, that's the point. Art makes things unnatural. Think about it. It's right. Tits, a nip and tuck, get 'em so they don't go south when I lie down and they stick out a bit more. Perhaps a little extra definition – that's bigger tits to you, sonny.

I'm gonna work on having someone else do it, though. Dr Kaye, he's this great genius. But he can't be that great – look at Jonathon. I mean, you could buy a better face at the butcher's than that. And, anyway, I don't like him. I don't want no one what I don't like poking about inside me. He's very ordinary to look at. Kind of quiet and neat. A dull old bloke, I suppose – you wouldn't guess he spends all day sloshing about in blood and, even worse, fat. He gives me the creeps. He gives me a pain, there – in the premonition place. It hurts me to think about him. Look. Dr Kaye – ouch. Dr Kaye – ouch. Dr Kaye – ouch! See? What's that all about, then?

My brain! Why do I think things like that? Poor old Dr Kaye, no one likes him . . .

Ouch!

We've been looking through these books to pick what I'm going to get. There's a book for everything. There's a book of noses, a book of tits, a book of smiles, a book of eyes. Imagine! You can get anything. Apparently, you can even get new willies and fannies. Yuck!

'You won't need that,' said Jonathon. 'That's for women who've had children.' Yeeew!

'And what about the willies?' I asked. 'Are those for men who've had children as well?'

'Every man wants a new one of those. And so does every woman,' he said, and all the blokes laughed like idiots.

Then he asked me what sort I preferred. I mean, who does he think he is? As if it's any of his business. As if I actually knew so many I could make a choice. And everyone looked at me as if they expected me to answer. Like he was being normal or something.

So there was a long pause while they waited for me to answer, which I didn't fill in for them.

(She nods firmly at the camera, reaches out and turns it off.)

Bernadette

Bernadette lives in Bristol these days in a large house in Clifton, paid for out of the money she saved during the ten years she worked for Jonathon Heat. The house, as she says, is far larger than anything she could have afforded if she hadn't had that job.

I met her in her garden, of which she was enormously proud. We sat under an arch of clematis and honeysuckle while she poured tea and served slabs of dense black fruit cake to me and a handful of other guests who had come along to say hello and hear Bernadette tell her story – not for the first time, I think. The clematis was out, there were daisies on the lawn. Bernadette smiled and spread her hands.

'Look at me!' she said, and she chuckled and shook her head. She obviously couldn't believe her good fortune, owning such a nice house in such a nice area, and never having to work again at the age of only fifty-five. Prior to working with Heat, she had spent her days in a little terrace in Moss Side that she'd never really expected to leave.

'But this is coming down in the world for you, isn't it, Bernie?' teased one of her friends, a smartly dressed Jamaican man perhaps a few years younger than Bernadette who turned out to be a minister at her church.

'Oh, I could live like a princess at Home Manor with Mr Heat,' said Bernadette. 'But this is me own house.' She smiled and wriggled in her chair. She looked across and beamed at me. 'It somehow makes the chairs that much softer,' she said, and leaned back in her chair and laughed silently at her own joke.

Bernadette was first employed at Home Manor Farm as a nurse to care for Heat after his various surgical procedures. They met at the Barbara Standford Clinic in Manchester, where Bernadette was employed as a ward sister – her first stint for the private sector after twenty years-plus for the National Health, something I got the impression she rather disapproved of herself for. Her husband had recently died, a number of frighteningly large debts had surfaced and earning more money became a priority. She met Heat only briefly when he attended to have an MRI scan – if he wasn't worrying about his looks, it was his health, according to Bernadette – and a few days later, a letter fell through her letter box offering her an interview at Home Manor Farm. When she got there, she was the only applicant.

'He really took a liking to me, I don't know why,' she said, and pulled a sad face. The fact was, she confessed, she felt she'd let Heat down. He had called her to his house, but his problems had not changed and the damage he was doing to himself had gone on unabated. She had changed nothing.

'I can't believe that you did anything but good in your time there,' said Patrick, the minister. 'It may be that saving him wasn't your purpose.'

Bernadette looked comforted by that thought and went on with her story.

She and Heat had a strong bond that got stronger over the years. Patrick actually suggested to me that Heat saw Bernadette as a mother figure and Dr Kaye as a father figure, and that the rift that developed between them echoed the rift that had occurred between his own mother and father when he was young. That I don't know, but it is true that Bernie has strong maternal qualities, and it would be typical of Heat to employ someone in that role.

Over the years she had a great deal of training at Heat's house – she attended courses in counselling and learned to help in theatre, too, to help with surgical procedures after Heat built an operating theatre in his own house. For a while she was closely involved with all the work done on him, but, as the work became increasingly experimental, Bernadette began to see Heat's obsession with surgery as an illness in itself. She did her best to get him to share her viewpoint, refusing to take part in the operations, although she still nursed him afterwards, but nothing she could do or say would turn Heat from his course. Even after his face collapsed, he still turned to Dr Kaye for help. To Bernadette, it was like a form of addiction, with Heat dependent on the very thing that was destroying him and Kaye as the supplier. But Heat also refused to get rid of her, despite pressure from Dr Kaye, although, increasingly, he found work for her away from the house.

When Bernadette first met Jonathon Heat, she thought of him as a kind of wounded saint, a man with the power to transform the lives of others, but, tragically, never his own. Yet, by the end, she'd come to believe that he'd led Sara into his own doom, deep into a mental illness in the disguise of treatment, and finally to an extreme form of self-harm, in which she was willing to sacrifice herself to feed his vanity.

'When I looked at Sara, I saw a beautiful young woman, everything a girl could ever want to be. But she saw nothing like that. She saw only ugliness. It was the same with Mr Heat, who was such a good-looking man when he was young. What Mr Heat did, he turned himself into what he saw in the mirror. And you know what? He was right. He'd become a monster, only he was so skilled with his lies, no one could ever have known. I thought I knew him so well, he was like a son to me. I never even guessed what was going on inside.'

Bernadette was at Home Manor Farm for only a week or so after Sara moved in, before she was due to fly out to Jamaica. She hated being answerable to Dr Kaye and had been seriously considering quitting her job. She felt that she was no longer earning her generous wages.

'The only way I was able to justify it,' she said, putting her chin up proudly, 'was by helping out the church.'

'Oh, Bernadette has always been able to spend money,' said the minister. He paused for her to look alarmed. 'With a little help from her friends.' And everyone leaned back and laughed.

As a matter of fact, Bernadette had already tried to resign several times, but so far Heat had always managed to talk her round. She was touched by his loyalty. But he always seemed to find something for her to do away from the house at the times when she felt that she might be useful. On this occasion, she felt as though her counselling skills might be helpful to Sara but, once again, she was being sent away. To her disgust, any counselling was to be done by Dr Kaye, which she felt was inappropriate. Heat was launching some initiatives back in her native Jamaica and Bernadette was going along for a holiday and to visit some friends and family for a few months. She didn't help with administration and organisation – those weren't her skills – but her signature was needed to release the money at various points along the way. No Bernadette, no money for good causes. In this way, her hands were tied. Sara's operation would take place while she was away in Jamaica. The idea was that she'd fly back afterwards to help nurse her while she was recovering.

Bernadette was suspicious of Sara at first, assuming that she was out of the same mould as so many of those who surrounded Heat – out for what she could get. But she soon decided that wasn't the case at all. Sara was a charming girl, full of life and high hopes, and without a speck of deception in her. That might seem an odd claim to make about someone who made so much up, but to Bernadette there was a big difference between fantasy and deception. She was well aware that Sara did not always tell the truth, sometimes on purpose – but never to self-serve or use others.

Bernadette rapidly fell under her spell. She felt that Sara was in many ways like Heat had been when she first met him – innocent, full of talent, but fighting the same demons. She was very anxious for a young girl moving into a house that she saw as inhabited by flatterers and deceivers, serving up disease under the guise of beauty. All her instincts warned her that Sara should not be living with Heat; all her professional training told her that she was not in a good mental state to have so much surgery done. The child was only seventeen years old! What did a beautiful young person want with being cut up like that? There was no sense to it.

And the mask-wearing scared her. After she moved to Home Manor Farm, Sara, who had almost stopped using masks until her accident with the iron, was rarely seen without it.

'You don't cover up your face unless you have something to hide,' said Bernadette. But what Sara was hiding, or hiding from, she never made up her mind.

During the few days she had before leaving, Bernadette made it her business to spend as much time with Sara as she could. She was frustrated that she was being sent away, and suspected this had been arranged by Heat and Kaye in order to pre-empt any trouble she might cause. If so, they were right. Even in the time she had, Bernadette did her best to convince Sara not to go ahead. A girl of her age and looks! She should at least wait for a while before rushing in . . .

Sara listened and smiled and promised to think about it, but Bernie was not convinced.

'I want you to think seriously about this, Sara. It's important.'

'Oh, but I've been thinking about it, Bernie – all my life,' said Sara.

So Bernadette was powerless. During the short time she had with Sara, her anxiety about what was going on got worse. A number of events, including the one related below, convinced her that no responsible doctor would let her go ahead with the surgery they were planning for her.

At this stage, she had not yet come to suspect Heat of any other motive than an overzealous desire to help.

Sara's mother, Jessica, was staying at Home Manor Farm during that first week of Sara's stay. Bernadette did not warm to Jessica – she thought her a cold woman and didn't think Sara liked her much either. Nevertheless, every morning, Sara got up at about ten and went down the corridor to visit her mother's room for breakfast. Sometimes Heat himself would join them. He seemed to expect this show of happy families.

Sara and her mother had invented a silly game, an exchange they played out every morning just for fun. On the very first morning of her stay, Heat had taken Jessica her breakfast in bed, a boiled egg and toast which he had prepared himself. Such gestures were typical of Heat. He had so many servants he could have ordered Jessica a banquet if he felt like it – but he went to the kitchen himself and boiled her an egg with his own hands, just to make her feel welcome

71

at his house. To many of the staff at Home Manor, it was the sort of thing that made them love him so dearly.

Sara walked in the door on the first day and found Heat sitting there on the edge of her mother's bed.

'Jonathon's made me breakfast in bed,' exclaimed Jessica, anxious that her daughter didn't think anything else had happened there.

'A boiled egg,' said Sara.

'Eaten with a silver spoon,' replied Jessica, waving her spoon, which was genuinely made of solid silver, in the air.

Jessica and her daughter had not been born with silver spoons in their mouths, as the saying goes, and Heat was delighted with the remark. Every day after that, he sent up a silver spoon with Jessica's breakfast, engraved with her initials for her to keep, to show that from now on, she would have a silver spoon in her mouth every day if she wanted it. Jessica later claimed she found the gifts a bit tiresome, and it's likely that Heat thought he was being far more generous than he was. He'd been so fabulously rich for so long, he no longer had any idea of the cost of things in the real world.

On this particular morning, Bernadette happened to be in the corridor when Sara opened her door. She stood still to watch as Sara's head popped out. But instead of turning towards Bernadette and her mother's room, as might be expected, Sara was looking the other way down the corridor. Whatever it was she was looking at must have been very interesting, even a little alarming, because she let out a slight but audible gasp and raised her hand to her throat. Even though Bernadette was standing slapbang in the middle of the corridor, Sara was so intent she didn't even notice her. That was odd, but what made the whole incident truly strange was that when Bernadette, who had a clear view over her shoulder, followed her eyes to see what she was looking at, the corridor was empty. For what felt like ages the two of them stood stock still, staring at nothing, Bernadette moving her head this way and that to try and work it out, but getting nothing. It was only when Tom Woods, the security chief, turned the corner and came walking along with that slightly splayed stride he'd acquired from too much time at the gym that Sara looked up and saw Bernadette watching her.

Their eyes met and held each other for a second or so; Bernadette raised her eyebrows in query.

Sara spread her hands like a magician, but she had nothing to show.

'Boo,' she hooted softly, behind her mask.

'Oh, boo, is that all?' said Bernadette, unimpressed.

Sara cocked her head to one side as if to say, 'Is that so?' Then she turned and carried on her way with no further comment.

'Boo to you, too,' growled Bernadette under her breath, cross at being fobbed off.

She watched Sara disappear into her mother's room, then made a call on her mobile to inform Heat that Sara was up. There was a treat in store for her that morning.

Bernadette had noticed the coolness between mother and daughter and wondered if Sara was jealous. In fact, she had reason to be. Unknown to her, Heat had already spent more than one night with Jessica. Despite his ruined looks, he still had his appeal. Heat behaved beautiful, and women responded as if he still was. Bernadette was used to juggling the intense sexual emotions that always surrounded Heat and had warned him that he might alienate Sara, who, even if she didn't know what was going on, would be aware of the tension one way or the other.

Heat decided to remedy the situation by serving Sara her breakfast in bed and by doing it in Jessica's room, in case the mother thought he was after the same with her daughter as he'd already had with her. Bernadette could see this going badly wrong, but Heat had ignored her warnings and gone ahead. Once he'd made up his mind on doing someone a favour, nothing on earth could stop him.

Ten minutes later, Heat arrived with the inevitable troop of staff who followed him around the house, one of them bearing a large breakfast tray. Bernadette joined the train. At the door, one person knocked while another handed Heat the tray. When Jessica called to come in, they all entered, one after the other, in a row, like soldiers.

Bernadette gives an hilarious account of that breakfast. With Heat and his entourage there were now no less than seven people in the room, four of them with nothing to do but watch Heat. They stood around awkwardly, not knowing where to put themselves. Jessica was furious. For one thing, the last time she had seen Jonathon was late the previous night, when he had been making love to her. He had somehow neglected to tell her about this little treat for her daughter the following morning. She was ruffled after a night's sleep, and her face was puffy and old-looking at the best of times in the morning, before she'd had time to attend to it. Not only that, but she was bursting for a pee but was unable to get herself out of bed since she was stark naked. Bernadette, who has a surprisingly wicked sense of humour, found this hilarious.

'And putting her clothes on under the sheets would have been too undignified for her,' she chortled.

Sara – somewhat cruelly, since she knew that Heat, too, had anorexic tendencies – insisted that he eat with her, despite his claim that he'd already had breakfast. The two sat down opposite one another at a little table in the window. Neither of them liked to eat in public and, at the end of the meal, Bernadette found buttered toast torn into pieces and cast onto the floor, where both of them had emptied their plates. The fact that they'd both used the same trick amused and appalled her.

In fact, as predicted, the supposed treat was embarrassing and bad-tempered, and Heat left as soon as he could, his entourage winding out behind him like a many-headed snake. Jessica sighed elaborately.

'That man has no sense sometimes!' she exclaimed. Sara glared at her, and Jessica decided not to pursue that thread, pulled on her gown and went to the bathroom to have her delayed wee, to shower and get herself ready for the day.

Heat had left Sara a brown paper bag on the table before he left, which she now tipped out to see what was in it. The bag was full of fruit and freshly peeled vegetables – healthy options, to encourage her to eat.

'Good grief,' growled Sara, who had been expecting something more exciting. Right at the bottom of the bag she found a big slice of carrot cake with butter icing on top. Heat thought that Sara loved carrot cake but he knew she would never ask for it openly, and so he had hidden it away in the hope that she might eat well when she was on her own.

Sara stared, fascinated, at it.

'Cake,' she said. 'Why does he think I want cake?'

'Because you told him you did,' pointed out Bernie.

Sara turned her masked face up to her. 'Oh! So I did,' she laughed. 'Poor Jonathon,' she said. 'He believes everything I tell him, and I never have the heart to tell him things he doesn't want to hear.'

'You and everyone else,' complained Bernadette. 'Maybe that's why he's such a mess.'

'He likes carrot cake. He smiled when I said I loved it, too. I made him happy.'

Bernadette snorted. 'It'll take more than cake to make him happy.'

Suddenly, to Bernadette's surprise, Sara stood up, pushed her mask back and kissed her on the cheek.

'Real lips for you, Bernie,' she whispered, and gave her a dazzling smile.

Bernadette herself smiled at the memory as she told this tale. 'She was full of love,' she declared. Full of love, and she never had a chance to let it out!' Discreetly, one of her friends handed her a box of tissues.

Sara wandered over to her mother's dressing table and began to idly pick up items of make-up. She tried a dab of eye pencil on her finger.

'Jonathon's so kind, isn't he?' she said.

'Well. He is, yes. But perhaps he's not very good at it,' suggested Bernie, and both she and Sara looked at each other and smiled.

'It's true, but I love him anyway,' said Sara stoutly. And it was true, Bernie could vouch for that. Sara's eyes lit up like candles whenever Jonathon was near.

'You and seven million other girls,' Bernie replied.

It was at this point that she remembered what had happened earlier in the corridor outside Sara's room. 'What were you looking at in the corridor this morning?' she asked. 'I was there the whole time. Didn't you see me?'

Sara put down the eye pencil with a clatter; the memory alarmed her. 'Didn't you see her?' she demanded.

'See who? There was no one there.'

Sara turned to look at her, then turned back to the mirror. 'A girl,' she said. 'I keep seeing her. I've never seen her up here before, though.'

'Who is it?'

'I don't know. I suppose she must be a ghost, if you can't see her. I don't think anyone else can, either.' Sara picked up a lip brush and leaned into the mirror. 'I recognise her from somewhere, which is really odd because she has no face. And another thing,' she added as she applied a thin red line round the lips of the mask she was wearing. 'You know what? The bitch was wearing my clothes.'

Sara said this quite casually, as if seeing faceless ghosts wearing your own clothes was commonplace, but her words filled Bernie with horror. Suddenly, that calm spring morning was full of foul work. Many times she herself had felt uneasy presences at Home Manor Farm. So far she had put these feelings down to her discomfort at the practices of Dr Kaye, but now that someone else had confirmed her suspicions she was struck with a sudden sense that the dead were suffering as well as the living in this house.

This conviction froze her to the spot. By the time she had gathered herself together to respond, Sara had left the room. Bernadette ran after her to carry on the conversation, but Sara had nothing more to say on the matter.

'You know what, Bernie? I don't think I believe in dead people,' she said. 'And, even if I did, there's not much we can do for them, is there?'

With that, she ended the conversation.

This exchange unsettled Bernadette so much that she spent the next few days trying to reschedule her trip to Jamaica. That Sara was having visions of a girl with no face wearing her own clothes just weeks away from cosmetic surgery was enough to alert anyone. But Heat insisted that only her signature would do to release the money, that it was too late to change things without serious consequences for the projects. All she could do was report her concerns to both Heat and Dr Kaye. She did this dutifully, but without any belief that it would do any good. Bernadette had never known Kaye consider anyone unfit for surgery in all the years she'd known him. She left for Jamaica in an anxious state of mind, a feeling that did not lessen as the days passed.

Mark

Sara had left her old life behind so unexpectedly there were gaps everywhere – at school, at home, in the bars where she once drank, the clubs where she'd danced. Heat had whisked her away to a world of private tutors and excellence that her old teachers could only dream about and a life of luxury that her friends and family could never attain. She was like a ghost to them already – a memory of someone who had passed on to a better place.

But some things money can't buy. A family, for instance, and friends – but perhaps that's not true. Sara had never been so popular as she was at Home Manor Farm. Everyone thought she was wonderful. Household staff, designers, entrepreneurs, producers and celebrities all courted her. Life was so busy she hardly had time to sit down. But Sara stayed in touch with Janet and one or two others from her old life. She called her new crowd 'fairground friends' – there was nothing behind the front. Janet came to see her as often as she was able, which was not that often since she was in the middle of her A-levels, and Heat, as jealous as ever, preferred

Sara to be on her own. When she did get out to Home Manor Farm, Heat took them on lavish shopping trips and to parties, but sooner or later they got back to doing what they had always done – slopping around in Sara's room, talking and watching TV.

And, of course, money can't buy you love.

According to Mark, it wasn't true that he'd asked her to take him back so that he could be the one to dump her. His version of the truth was simpler: he just didn't go back with her after she jilted him that last time.

'She was always chucking me over,' he said. 'It did me in. Then after a few days she'd ring up as if nothing had happened and things were going to go on just the same. That time she rang up and said, "When are we seeing each other?" and I said, "We're not."'

They'd hurt each other, as lovers do. But now he was missing her.

Sara had never been an easy person to go out with. She was so volatile – she could be all over him one moment, and then hardly seem to know he existed the next. But she swore she adored him, and the truth was, in his heart, Mark knew it was true. They had a connection. There were times with her when all sense of the other disappeared, when it wasn't like being with another person at all, but as if they were one person in two bodies. And he lusted after her like a dog for a bone. It made him dizzy. All in all, Sara was the most delightful thing that had ever happened to him.

On the other hand, she scared him. She was scarcely a sensible choice for a girlfriend. Her anorexia, the accidents, her soaring ambition, great strength and terrible fragility all meant she was as likely to head for disaster as glory – perhaps both. It made him want to care for her, but the idea of looking after someone like Sara was a joke in itself. She had no conception of her own weakness. She seemed to see her elements of self-destruction as actual strengths.

He didn't hear about the accident with the iron until after she'd left hospital, but, when he did, he was mortified. It had happened only a week or so after they'd separated and although she'd always fiercely denied doing any kind of harm to herself, he was sure she had. Any number of times before then he'd almost given her a call, but he held off simply because ... he wasn't sure why. Because a part of him truly did want it to be over and he was scared it would start up again. Because she thrilled him and excited him, but scared him, too. Because he was going to university the next year after a gap year, it would all fall apart then anyway, surely ...

And it hurt. Being with Sara hurt.

When he heard that she'd been whisked away by Jonathon Heat, it made his hair stand on end. She had moved so far away from him, that was partly it. But Sara was like a glass rocket fired at the moon – she might actually get there but surely she'd shatter to a million pieces on impact. Jonathon Heat! In an instant, he realised how close Heat could get to her, how dangerous he was for her – how alike their madness was.

He rang Jessica, but he didn't get any sense out of her – she was very cool with him. He got the impression she blamed him for Sara's accident, which made sense because he blamed himself. She did, however, tell him about the planned operations.

Mark's heart sank. His premonitions were all true. 'I thought you were against that,' he said.

'It's for her scars,' said her mother.

'Is that all?' he asked, with a sinking feeling.

'She's having a few other things done while she's in theatre. Jonathon was willing to pay for it, why not?'

Jonathon! The man with a hundred faces; the man with no face. He was the last person on earth Mark would have wished on Sara. Jessica spoke the name as if it was a piece of chocolate cake.

'But Jonathon Heat is mad, everyone knows that,' said Mark.

'He's treating her very well, that's all I know,' said Jessica. 'Goodbye, I must run.' And she put the phone down smartly.

Mark dithered for a while longer. He rang Janet, but she was away. He wanted to call Sara, but . . . things had changed. All that wealth and celebrity! She wouldn't want to hear from a blast from the past like him. In the end, love and worry got the better of him. He pressed her name on his mobile – and there she was, on the other end of the line, as if she was sitting next door; as if it was still only yesterday.

'I was terrified; I was certain she'd be as cold as ice, but you know what?' he told me. 'She was pleased to hear from me. She was really happy I rang. She'd been wanting to ring me up as well. I was so relieved. I remember, after I put the phone down, thinking, Wow – now I'm happy! It took me by surprise, how happy she made me just by wanting to hear from me. I caught sight of myself in the mirror and I had this big soppy smile over my face.' And he pulled his face into an imitation of his big soppy face – in love up to his eyeballs.

Within a minute of hearing from him, Sara was making plans. She wanted Mark to come up and work at Home Manor Farm.

'But I've got a job,' he said.

'Pizza Hut,' she said.

'Yeah, and?'

'Well, what do you think? There's no comparison.'

'But what's the job?'

'I don't know. He said if any of my friends wanted a job up here he'd find them one. He's always doing that sort of thing – he's really generous.'

Mark almost sneered, but he bit his tongue.

'You and him,' he said.

'What?'

'Well. You know.'

'No, I don't know. What do you mean?'

'Are you . . . an item?'

'Me and Jonathon Heat?' Sara just laughed. 'You must be joking! He's ancient. And he's falling to bits.'

'It said in the papers . . .'

'The papers! Mark, come on!'

There were any number of stories about Sara and Heat in the celebrity mags. The one Mark was thinking about was a distance shot of Sara and Heat with their masked faces pushed together. She had one leg up on his hip, which he was holding under the knee. There were a number of other pictures of the two of them in varying degrees of closeness, but that was the one that had got to Mark.

'That picture of you and him kissing.'

'We weren't kissing. We were wearing masks. You can't kiss in a mask. Listen, Mark, there was no mouth-to-mouth contact, OK?'

'It looked pretty close to me.'

'He poses them. It's fun. We set stuff up for the cameras and then get caught. It's just fun.'

'I bet he thinks it is.'

'Well, I suppose he likes the idea that he can still cop off with someone like me. It's like a game. But, yuck! Can you imagine? No thanks!'

'I know we split up,' said Mark, and he waited a little bit for Sara to contradict him, but she didn't. 'I'd just find it pretty difficult if you and him were together, you know?'

'Well, we're not.'

Mark took a deep breath. 'Can I think about it?'

'Sure. Then say yes.'

'Go on, then, yes.'

'Yes! Great! Oh, Mark, we're going to have *fun!*'

Sara sorted it out the same day. Heat offered Mark a job in security, and Mark drove down to Cheshire the day after that.

On his way down from Manchester to Home Manor Farm, on the edge of the Peak District, Mark began to feel more and more anxious. Thoughts buzzed around his mind like flies. For a start, why hadn't Sara told Heat that she and Mark had been lovers, just that he was an old school friend down on his luck? She'd claimed she didn't want to make Heat jealous. So what was all that about, if there was supposed to be nothing between her and Heat?

Then there was Heat's fame and wealth – that was scary stuff. How do you behave to someone you already know through newspapers, music and film, and all the hundreds of stories and jokes you'd heard about them? It was almost as if Heat had somehow ceased to be human any more. Ridiculous, of course, but that was how Mark felt about it.

By the time he was driving through the actual grounds, Mark was feeling extremely weird. Home Manor Farm itself, of course, was as weird as every mad rock star's country home should be. On first impression it was an ordinary old country park, landscaped centuries ago, tended and farmed and looked after as much for pleasure as profit for generations. There were the deer grazing in herds, the oak trees spreading their arms wide, the leaves neatly levelled above the cropped pasture by the grazing animals. There was the lake lying quietly in its hollow, the plantings, the avenues of limes, the shrubs and gardens. But then you'd look up and see a giraffe grazing on the tree tops, or a row of blue and yellow cherry trees, or a red lawn, or a giant hand made of aluminium. Around every corner were sculptures. Heat seemed to have a weakness for giant broken figures, statues with the arms fallen off or their heads cracked open. In one field the cows grazed among a scattered wreckage of giant household tools – colanders, saucepans, knives and forks, potato mashers and so on – all over ten metres long, lying rusting in the grass.

And then the house itself. Calling it a farm was a joke. It was a stately home. It was just enormous. All that money, all that fame. It made Mark feel like little Jack crawling up to the door of a giant.

Inside, he was asked to wait in the library. He was half expecting to find an old-fashioned country house library as he was shown in – walls lined with leather-bound books, steps on rusty wheels, cobwebs hanging in the corners.

But it'll probably be a butterfly house or a cattery or a recording studio, thought Mark. The flunky who had greeted him opened the door for him. There was a blast of cool air – the air conditioning was working overtime in there – and, to his surprise, inside was just as he had first thought. Books. Only the cobwebs were missing. The library, like the rest of Heat's house, was spotless.

Mark wandered up along the shelves, looking for something to read. It was a collection of leather-bound books, smelling of age, just as they should. He hauled out a huge old volume and opened it on a table. It was full of maps. He found the year 1701 on one of them. From what he could make out, it was a book of handdrawn maps of the Indian Ocean.

'You should be wearing these,' said a voice behind him.

Mark whirled round. Standing behind him, holding out a pair of spotless white cotton gloves, was Jonathon Heat himself.

'Sorry... sorry. I mean, no one said,' gasped Mark, who had not heard him enter and was taken completely by surprise.

He waited for Heat to speak again, but it wasn't Heat who had spoken at all. Standing behind him were two men in sharp black suits.

'That's all right, sir, I'll deal with it,' said one of the men, in the voice that Mark had thought was Heat's. The man took the gloves deferentially off Heat and went to close the book, carefully dusting it and inspecting it for damage before he did so.

Mark grimaced at Heat. 'Sorry, I didn't know they were so valuable,' he said. Heat still didn't reply. He stood perfectly still, his head slightly to one side, watching Mark from behind his mask as if he could see inside his mind and know what his purpose was in being here before he did anything so rash as giving away his voice.

Like many other people, Mark found his first meeting with Heat somewhat surreal. Heat was dressed in a frock coat and a pair of jeans embossed with a paisley pattern, and a wide blue denim tie with a picture of the dying Christ on it. It was exactly the sort of thing he wore on stage – and this was just his housewear.

'People are always going on about celebrities and the clothes they wear,' said Mark later. 'I always thought it was all really shallow and ridiculous, but, when I saw it, the clothes really were something. He looked like he'd been gift-wrapped, it was all so perfect – the fit, the cloth, everything. It was really odd, like we were on stage or in some sort of a film.'

But the strangest thing was the mask. Not being able to see the man's face made him unreadable, of course, as if Heat had turned himself into some sort of robot – a robot with feelings, but unknowable, unreadable feelings. And the mask itself. Its texture was so much like skin that the first thing Mark thought when he saw it, like Sara, was that maybe it was genuinely made from real human skin.

There had been a lot of speculation about that mask and its provenance. Like a great many other things in Heat's possession, it was lost to the fire some weeks later.

Heat stood there for a long time, looking at him as if he was something in a tank. Mark flushed and failed to meet his eye, but then he thought, Shit! He's just another guy, and he looked straight back, through the mask holes and into his face.

Heat didn't wait so long that it was going to be a standoff. He nodded at the man who was putting the book back, then took a couple of steps forward towards Mark, so that he was just a little too close. Mark could smell him – expensive cologne, antiseptic and a faint whiff of decay.

'I hope you're going to be nice to her,' said Heat.

'Yes, of course I am,' said Mark, in a voice that, to his disgust, was rather too high. He wondered how much Heat really knew about their relationship.

Heat nodded, then turned and walked off. No hello, no goodbye. He'd simply been delivering his orders.

'There,' said one of the suits behind him, in a tone of satisfaction. 'Mr Heat always likes to welcome his new employees. This way, sir.' He turned and led the way out of the library and up the stairs.

Poor Mark was feeling very shaky now. Was Sara going to be horrible to him, too? What had she said to Heat to make him behave in such a way? But he needn't have worried. She ran at him as soon as he was through the door, wrapped her arms round him and buried her head in his neck.

'You came, you came, it's so great that you came,' she said. Mark's heart swelled. He thought, Ain't life grand, that you can be made to feel like a king just because someone's glad to see you? He lifted her off the ground and gave her a big fat hug.

After they'd said their hellos, Sara immediately launched into all the things she was doing – modelling with Tiffany Gray, acting lessons, singing lessons, dancing lessons, the lot. It sounded fantastic. She seemed blissfully happy at that point, which made Mark feel a little sad. She was moving beyond him. He had never been sure how much of her ambitions were pie in the sky, but now that they were coming true he felt that they were making him somehow more unreal.

When she started on about the surgery, his feelings must have shown on his face, because she shrugged impatiently.

'That's what you have to do these days,' she said.

Mark shrugged back. 'Dummies are made of plastic, dummy, not people,' he said.

'Don't call me a dummy, dummy,' she said, and laughed.

Mark knew he should keep his mouth shut, but he couldn't help it.

'I just think...' he began.

'It's not your business any more,' she told him.

'As a friend, as a friend I think it's a bad idea.'

Defiantly, Sara started going through the list. Mark listened with increasing alarm. Her chin, her nose, her eyebrows. Then she went on about her boobs. It just made him see red.

'You idiot,' he said.

'I guess, somehow, I thought they were mine,' he said later.

'It isn't any of your business any more,' she repeated angrily.

'You lose feeling in your nipples,' he told her weakly, half smiling.

'Now, that *really* isn't any of your business any more,' Sara said again. She looked as if she didn't know whether to laugh or get cross. Mark absolutely didn't want to row so soon, so he did what he often did on those occasions: he made her laugh.

He gestured at her boobs and said, 'But they a-make-a me a-feel-a like a man,' in a heavy Italian accent. Sara smiled, he held out his arms and gave her another hug, quick, before the moment went. They stood like that, front to front, for rather longer than they needed to. Mark found himself glancing across at that big double bed, thinking, Well, would they?

Sara followed his eye and laughed. She stepped back.

'Jonathon would be furious if he found out,' she said.

'I thought you weren't doing anything with him.'

'No way! He doesn't even fancy me, anyway. He's nice – like your dad or something. Protective. just because he's a rock star doesn't mean to say he wants to shag everyone he meets.'

'Doesn't it?'

'No!'

Then why'd he be so cross?'

'Oh, he gets jealous anyway. Just on principle. He's really protective. He's just a bit damaged, you know.'

Mark touched the triangular scar on her cheek. She looked at him defiantly.

'Oh, crap,' she said. 'It was an accident, how many times do I have to tell people?' She got cross about it. 'I keep telling people, I don't do that.'

So she said. So she always said.

By and large, it was a happy reunion. That evening, they had dinner with Jonathon and Bernadette, who was leaving the next day, and Heat was as nice as pie. You'd never guess that he had been almost threatening earlier that day. Instead, he told them stories about being famous, about music, about his remarkable life and the remarkable people he'd met. He parted with Mark on good terms, although he made it clear he was going to be kept busy.

'I give a good deal here, Mark, but you have to work for it.'

'I can work hard,' said Mark.

'There's a lot to do. We're having a big party, you know about that? We're going to give Sara a proper launch. You won't know her by the time we're done. I've taken some staff off security to help out. Tom'll need a lot of overtime from you, I expect.'

Mark glanced across at Sara to see how she'd react to maybe not seeing so much of him. She smiled fondly and gave nothing away.

The next day, Mark was introduced to his new boss, Tom Woods, and began work at Home Manor Farm.

Sara — 23 May 2005

(Sara is sitting cross-legged in her four-poster with the curtains drawn. She's wearing a Jonathon Heat mask made up to look totally furious, with drawn-down eyebrows, sparks and flashes flying out of the eyes and an ugly scowl over the mouth. The mask is heavily covered with make-up and decorated with plastic flies, dirty tinsel and a transfer of a fat lady.)

It's off, Jonathon Heat. Bloody wandering hands old man, take your face off with one of his kisses. On the record, his breath smells. That's one thing. You get little whiffs of air from under that mask. That's another.

Let's not go there.

He can't help being disgusting, but what's really disgusting is being unfair. He's cancelled our gig. After all that work! All that time going through the moves with me. I bet he was just rehearsing all the time. Him, him, him. Or he thinks I'm actually useless, no talent at all, and he's just doing it to be kind, like he does things to be kind to kids. You know, giving them days out at the zoo or throwing parties for them or giving money to charity. That's me – I'm a charitable cause. Please give generously, utterly pathetic. Thinks she can sing. Sara has been suffering from delusions of being able to entertain. Try not to wince or pull faces. Be generous – talentless. Twat, please help.

(She cries, holding her face in her hands.)

We were *brilliant.* I have the video. Well, actually, that's another thing, I don't have the video. He told me yesterday the other copies had been damaged and he needed to have a look at the one I had and now I haven't got it back. Accident. Guess what? He dropped it in the bath! Can you believe that? I don' fink so, Charlie. Bastard. He was worried someone might pirate it, and who might that someone be? Charitable Charlie – me! That's how much he trusts me. But I don't care about that. What I care about is . . . big party, everyone coming, all the stars. You know about his parties, you read about them in magazines. Everyone comes. Imagine doing a duet with Jonathon Heat in front of all *them* – you'd be mega overnight! Everyone'd be talking about you, everyone'd wonder who you are. And I wasn't bad! I mean, I'm not as good as him – he's been going for years – but I have a really nice voice. Everyone says so. I move well. I have a good body. Oh! Maybe that's it. I'm too fat. Too ugly – but for God's sake, how can you be ugly with a mask on? Even I can't be ugly with a mask on! It must be fat, then. Fat twat, that's me.

(She lifts up her face and gnashes her teeth — literally. It's a half-joke, but there are tears sparkling in her eyes.)

His advisers warned him that doing a set with a girl as young as me, who was about to undergo surgery at his house, might lead to some nasty publicity. Oh, dear me, nasty publicity, oh no, can't have that. Please, no publicity for Mr Heat, he doesn't like it, you know. It makes him break out in dimples.

Maybe it's true. Someone like him has to be careful. Look what happened to Michael Jackson. He does have to be careful. And maybe the vid did get damaged. Or maybe he's just paranoid...

And it's always his advisers. Never him, he never says no to anything. His advisers just keep stopping him, poor old Jonathon! Crap. No one would have seen my face under the mask. We'd have made a right pair.

(She laughs.)

I was looking forward to it, though.

(She puts her hands to her face and cries, then in a fit of anger starts beating the pillows.)

Bastard shitbag bloody bloody bloody. Arghghghgh!

(Sara grabs hold of a mirror and stares at her face. She begins to draw a jagged red line on the mask with an eyeliner pencil, which she then throws across the bed.)

95

There's something you should know. I'm being spied on! Everywhere. Here in my room. I can't do anything. Every day I search this bed from top to bottom for bugs. You think I'm mad. I think I'm mad. But I don't know, do I? That's the thing. I don't know…

(She carries on painting the face before glancing again at the camera and reaching over to turn it off.)

The Party

Once he stopped being a guest and became a member of staff, Mark barely saw Sara. Heat, on the other hand, saw her all the time. They worked out together, they went to restaurants together, they went shopping together. They were even getting massaged together. Mark knew this because Sara kept in touch by phone and text. She never said who she was with, just where she was, but who else would be with her at Tiffany Gray's, or having lunch in Paris, or eating at Heathcote's or shopping at Vivienne Westwood? Heat must have bought her half the clothes in Manchester from what she said. The only times Mark saw her was somewhere in the distance, having a good time with Jonathon Heat. It was eating him up.

He'd been telling himself that he and she could be just good friends, but that's not what his heart was saying. Even if she wasn't sleeping with Heat, the fact that she preferred to hang out with him hurt. He kept telling himself it was all a career move on Sara's part and he couldn't blame her for that. Who wouldn't prefer to eat out at the best restaurants, stay at five-star hotels, hang out with the stars – but it still hurt. He was spending his days walking about, hurting.

The job Heat had given him had actually turned out to be rather good. The security system at Home Manor Farm was one of the most sophisticated available and poor old Tom Woods, who ran security, had no idea. He was an old-fashioned sort of guy who liked to walk up and down the corridors at night with a torch, or sit in a box with a Thermos and a TV, and keep half an eye on the CCTV. He hadn't a clue about programming the system. Once the software was set up, he just left it to its own devices, running the CCTV, and operating the lights and a few doors from the central server; but that machine could pretty well run the house on its own if it was programmed properly. It didn't just control the security side of things. The whole electrical side of the house was on board as well.

Mark started off with routine jobs, patrolling the grounds and filing records, that sort of thing; but his subject at university was going to be computing and he was just dying to get his hands on that mainframe. There was a problem, though – Woods was against it.

Jonathon Heat and Tom Woods went way back. Woods had started out as a roadie in the early days when Heat was front man for the boy band Loose Trade. Heat usually went along with whatever Tom wanted, and Tom wanted the security server left well alone. For one thing, having no idea how it worked or what it could do, he mistrusted it deeply; his instinct was to let it alone in case it resented being disturbed. For another, he hated being shown up for an ignoramus and Mark's burst of enthusiasm when he saw the machine indicated that exactly that was on the cards. On this occasion, though, with a little help from Sara, Heat overruled him. Woods insisted that thing would go wrong, that a little knowledge was a dangerous thing, but Mark had the machine turning the lights on and off in fancy patterns, and making the cameras follow people up and down the corridors like a chameleon's eye in the first few hours. Woods hated him for it, and Mark had made an enemy right off. But he didn't care – he was having a great time. Within a day he was already able to manipulate the cameras individually and turn infrared tracking on and off all over the house – something that Woods didn't even know existed.

Neither Heat nor Woods could have realised the power this gave Mark, however. He could already track down where anyone was in the house, and spy on them, if he wished. And he did wish – but he was too honest. In fact, it took all his willpower not to spy on Heat and Sara. It wasn't any of his business. He didn't like the thought of what he might see.

The rest of the job consisted of walking about the grounds, keeping an eye on things, checking windows and so on. It was easy work, the pay was brilliant – but was it enough to pay for the heartache? Mark was feeling humiliated and lonely, and within a couple of weeks he was already thinking of packing the job in and going home. On the other hand, there was the big party coming up: that, Mark did not want to miss. It was all hands to the pumps when Heat threw a party, and he had been asked to help out on the night, serving food. He had already been given his costume and told the order of events. Heat's parties were planned with military precision to look spontaneous.

Mark decided to stay for the do and then give in his notice the next day. Apart from anything else, there was a chance, even if it was a small one, that he could see Sara and tell her goodbye.

The party, despite being held in secret, was of course well known to the press already, and on the night the paparazzi were out in force, hanging off the fence and climbing up trees to snap celebrities arriving. Heat's grooming of Sara was also supposed to be a secret, but the news got out about that, too, and Heat felt compelled to make a press statement in which he emphasised that he was looking into what could be done to help her, and that they were just friends. Sara was furious; as far as she was concerned she was there to be made a star, not be helped – as if she was sick – as if she needed help! She told Janet she thought Heat had orchestrated the whole leak in order to cut her out and was disgusted with the whole thing. It wasn't her launch any more. In a sneaking way, step by step, it had turned into yet another demonstration of how wonderful Jonathon Heat was.

Heat's parties were things of fable, and this one was no exception. The food was like a medieval banquet – a giant swan, two metres high, carved out of ice, chickens put together so they looked like lizards, a chocolate cake that weighed fifty kilos covered in chocolate masks, salmon arranged so that they looked like a shoal swimming up the tables, salads like Kew Gardens and sweets and bonbons from all over the world. The rooms were decorated with huge floral extravaganzas; there was live music from bands such as Antwerp, Maverick, the Serious Slits, the Lovely Girls and Bay Moon. Everyone dressed like catwalk princes and princesses, and major celebrities mingled with Sara's friends and family like long-lost relatives everyone had seen before only in pictures. They were nice to Sara and her friends, even the ones who hated the common public. Heat had seen to that.

Sara enjoyed the star-spotting, but she was embarrassed by the kind of attention she was getting. All the celebs were going out of their way to be nice to her, but not as one of them. She was another charity fan Jonathon had taken under his wing.

'They're all treating me as if I was normal,' she complained to Janet. Her friends and family were also embarrassing her by getting louder and louder as they got drunk, pointing out each new famous face with shrieks of excitement, which they tried unconvincingly to hush up. Several of them were trying to take photographs in secret – unplanned photos were strictly banned – and there was always a huge cluster of them gathered around the food tables like 'a crowd of overdressed maggots', as Sara put it.

Mark had been safely imprisoned behind one of the long tables, and by the time the party was half over, he'd barely even glimpsed Sara. He could see snatches of her through the crowds, and some of their mutual friends had come across to talk. Heat obviously suspected that there was more to him and Sara than he was being told and was keeping Mark well out of the way. He'd even had words with him a few days before, after catching him pausing in the corridor to talk to her.

'I don't ask for much considering the advantages you get working here, Mark, but . . .' he said. And he launched into a polite but angry suggestion that staff, meaning Mark, stay away from guests, meaning Sara.

Yes sir no sir your bony arse sir! Mark was furious. He complained about it to Sara on her mobile – one way Heat could not keep tabs on him – but she didn't seem to mind. Heat was jealous, he was used to getting his own way, he was just like a little kid, Mark was not to mind him, she said. And so Mark thought she didn't care that he wasn't seeing anything of her.

At about half past nine, Cheyenne from the Lovely Girls got up on a chair and announced that after a huge amount of nagging, she'd finally managed to convince Heat to do a set for his guests. Everyone clapped, cheered and laughed – they all knew this had been planned for weeks.

'Put on your masks!' shrieked Cheyenne. Staff appeared at the entrances carrying boxes of Heat masks. Everyone had to have their face covered while Heat recreated the famous opening act of the Night of the Mask Tour – 'Who We Baby'. The staff had already been issued with theirs, so they did not have to mingle or push in with the guests. Mark had been given one along with everyone else; but he had other plans. It was his last night at Home Manor Farm – he had nothing to lose. He had his own little game to play tonight and he wanted Sara to be able to recognise him if she saw him.

The masks were handed out, the lights went down, the spotlight focused on the middle of the floor, and Heat came on, wearing his flat cap, his blue pashmina, his short leather jacket and began to perform.

> 'This boy is not your man,
> This boy is a lonely child,
> What you see is what you get.
> Wear me, be me, eat me.
> Behind my face my secret thoughts
> Are there for all to see.
> Who we is
> Is who I am.
> You and me is
> All there is.'

No one was allowed to stay away while Heat performed, even the staff, and everyone had been instructed to leave their places and go to watch the show. But Mark held back, peering over the heads towards the spotlit area where Heat was doing his stuff. Not bad for an old bloke, he thought. In fact, it was quite mesmerising. But, to his eyes, there was someone more mesmerising still. He knew she was angry about being left out of this at the last moment. Maybe now he could ease up to her and say his goodbyes. Or – it was there in his mind still – perhaps she'd find a way to convince him to stay on.

Sara was standing at the back of the crowd, peering between the heads. It was dark, she was wearing her mask and clothes he'd never seen before, but he knew her so well – how she stood, how she moved, how she held her head – he'd know her anywhere. She looked as lovely as ever in his eyes, even from behind. Mark waited a moment, ready to duck under the table to go to her, but suddenly she turned round as if she'd felt the pressure of his eyes on her. She cast Heat one more quick glance, then turned, left the crowd and made her way over to his table.

On the spur of the moment, Mark decided to pretend not to know her.

'Can I get you anything, madam?' he asked, tipping his head to one side.

Sara frowned. 'You're not wearing a mask,' she said.

'Yes, I am,' he said.

'Where?'

'Here.' Mark touched the edges of his face and showed her what he'd done. He was right – he was wearing a mask, but he'd cut the face of it away, so that only the edges of it remained, and his own face was naked in the middle.

Sara laughed out loud; it was just the kind of thing she loved. 'That's not a mask!' she said.

'It's a mask-mask.'

'What's a mask-mask?'

'A mask that masks another mask.'

'And where's the other mask, then?'

Mark looked suspiciously from side to side like it was a big secret, then lifted up the cut-away and tapped his own face.

'Here.'

Sara laughed. 'God, you don't want to go out in public wearing that thing, that's awful. I'd take it back to the shop if I was you.' Mark smiled and there was a pause. They stood watching each other from opposite sides of the table.

'Don't I know you from somewhere?' she said at last.

Mark's heart did a quick bang-bang-bang. They used to play this game of not knowing each other and it usually led to seduction.

He ducked his head deferentially. 'I don't think so, madam. I only work here.'

'You're bad. You'll get the sack if they catch you.'

He shrugged, then glanced up at her. 'Why don't you take your mask-mask off and show me the real mask underneath?'

'What? Not here,' said Sara, as if taking off her mask was like going naked. Mark's eyes drifted away from Sara's face and down her body. She was wearing a designer dress, the kind of thing she'd never have been able to afford before. Mark had never really seen the point of spending so much money on clothes, but then he'd only ever seen people wearing such things in photos. In the flesh, it was different. It didn't so much reveal what was underneath, or even let on what was underneath, but somehow it really made him want to find out. They were clothes to take off.

He looked back up at her and smiled. She didn't say anything, just watched him. She was popping salad leaves into her mouth, slipping them under her mask. Mark thought, Hmm...underneath. Taking that mask off and kissing her – that would be like undressing her, too.

He was suddenly tongue-tied. Sara always filled him with desire. Now it was worse than ever, but it made him feel clumsy and inadequate.

Sara lifted up her arms. 'Do you wanna dance?' she asked.

'I can't.'

'Why not?'

He shrugged. 'I'm staff.'

'So what?'

'Staff aren't allowed to dance with Saras. Orders.'

Sara shrugged and waited.

'We could dance somewhere else,' he suggested.

'They keep watch all the time. We'd have to be entirely on our own.'

Mark's heart went bang-bang again. They were talking about something else, another kind of dance, one that usually doesn't happen standing up.

'If we were on our own,' he said carefully, 'would you dance with me then?'

'How could we be on our own?' she said. 'They have cameras everywhere.'

'If the cameras were off.'

'Ah, but how would we know they were off?'

'I'd know. I'm security, remember?'

'I'd have to know, too.'

Mark thought about it, and then said, 'If we were on our own in the dark, the cameras wouldn't see us then.'

Sara, he thought, panted very slightly. Perhaps her jaw just dropped slightly. He wasn't sure. You couldn't see under that mask. But he was pretty sure.

'On our own in the dark? What sort of a dance would it be?'

Mark smiled. 'That depends. We wouldn't have long.'

'Not a very long dance, then.'

'Sorry, not at first,' he said. 'I'd need some practice. I haven't done it for a bit.'

They'd entered a little intense world of their own, but now it was broken by applause as Heat finished his set. Sara turned and watched. Heat was looking around for something as he bowed: her.

'Maybe if we were on our own and in the dark I'd dance with you,' she said. 'Maybe not. I don't know. But it won't happen, will it?' She smiled ruefully and left to go and join in the applause before Heat missed her.

Heat was surrounded by people, but, as Sara suspected, he was waiting for her. He pulled her into the circle with him and pressed his mask to hers as if kissing while the cameras flashed. It was something he'd often done before but this time there was a brief touch of a tongue as he poked it through the mouth holes and touched her lips. No one had seen, it was so quick and secret. Then Heat turned away and was swallowed up by the crowd.

It was the first time he had kissed her like that. Done there in the full glare of the public, but in secret – it was typical Heat. His mask was beautiful, but she could never forget what lay underneath. And so close after her encounter with Mark... She had to fight an urge to wipe her lips at once.

Then the power went down. Suddenly, the whole room was plunged into darkness – lights, sound, the fountains of wine and chocolate all stopped. There was a minute of confusion.

'Everyone stay still, please. We'll have this fixed in a few minutes,' called a voice. Patches of torchlight appeared as staff began to find their way around. Sara didn't notice one among them that came on and off as it approached her until someone touched her elbow.

'Dance?' said a voice.

'Oh. It's you!'

Mark took her by the hand.

'Chance is a fine thing,' he whispered. But chance it never was.

Hidden in the dark confusion, Mark led her across the ballroom, out of the double doors at the other end and down a slope, towards the service area under the house. Heat had a labyrinth hidden down there where he stored his old props and costumes, and housed the security room, the boiler room and so on, and offices for his staff. Sara had never been down there before. There were rumours about passages going far out under the grounds to various outhouses and so on, so that Heat could travel underground all over the estate.

Through a solid-looking oak door, down a passage, through a pair of double doors . . . Now they entered another realm, under the house, lit by dull strips overhead.

'There's a back-up system down here,' said Mark. He stopped and looked at her. They were alone now. He wanted to kiss her, but she still wore her mask. He was unable to read her face at all.

'Dance now?' he asked.

'We're alone, but it's not dark,' said Sara.

Mark took a couple of steps to one of the doors and opened it. It was a cupboard. He took her hand; she followed him inside and shut the door behind them.

'It is now,' he said. He touched her bare arms. Even though they were alone, in the dark, even though she had come with him and shut the door, he still wasn't sure. The mask was confusing him.

They stood so close. It felt gorgeous. Mark slid his hands down to her waist.

'Is it dark enough now?' he whispered.

'What sort of dance?' she whispered back.

He touched her face – but there was no face, just the mask. 'I want to see you,' he said.

'It's too dark.'

'I have a torch.'

'I never take my mask off any more.'

That wasn't true – not quite. She almost always had it on these days, but she had been bare-faced when he had first seen her at Home Manor Farm. Bare-faced for him, he realised, since she was always masked when she was with Heat.

'The darkness is a mask,' he said. He was sure that, underneath, she was smiling at that.

She opened the door just a fraction, enough for a little light to get in, and stood there, waiting. Mark lifted his hands to the mask, paused, then lifted it up. There was her lovely face smiling up at him. It made his heart stand still. He wanted to tell her that he loved her, but he didn't dare.

She leaned up to him to kiss.

About five minutes later, the light coming in through the door grew brighter. The power was back on.

'I better get back,' said Sara.

'Can we meet again?' he asked.

'You want to see more of me?' she said. 'I don't think there's any more of me to see.'

Mark looked at her curiously, because nothing like that had happened. They had only kissed and stroked each other. She meant she had shown him her face; she meant she had shown him herself, but he didn't understand. She pulled a funny face and stepped outside. Mark followed. She put her mask back on, looked over her shoulder at him and smiled – he could see the sides of her face move. She turned to go, but then stopped suddenly. He could hear her gasp. She was looking forward along the corridor, but when he followed her eye line, there was nothing there.

'What is it?' he asked.

'Do you see her? There!'

Mark looked, but saw nothing.

'There she goes, round the corner and off home to bed,' she said in a quiet voice. She sounded very calm. 'Now, I wonder what that means?' she said. Then, before he could say another thing, she ran up the slope to the double doors and disappeared.

Jonathon Heat

(The following is an extract from a newspaper article written by Heat from prison.)

Stories about me are almost always not true. It was that way even before I was famous. People circulate damaging stories about me. It's a form of vandalism. People always want to break and deface beautiful things.

My motives with Sara were always pure. I never had any desire to sleep with her and I made no attempts to have sexual contact with her during the whole time she stayed at my house. Most especially, I had no designs to steal her beauty. Of course I'd heard of face transplants. It's not true that I ever denied that. And of course I hope one day to be fortunate enough to have one myself. But knowing about something and wanting something are different from abusing a position of trust in order to make it happen.

As soon as I saw her in hospital that day, I recognised a kindred spirit, someone with the same kind of talents and the same kind of problems. Yes, Sara and I are both ill in a way that no one can imagine unless they suffer from it themselves. Our illness is a strange thing. We are unable to recognise ourselves. I believe that one day our illness will become accepted as such by the medical profession.

When a normal person looks in the mirror they see a face and they know it's theirs. When Sara and I look in the mirror, we see a stranger. Dr Kaye took advantage of that situation and over the years encouraged me to have more and more surgery, setting me on an endless search for the identity I never had until, in the end, there was nothing of me left to recognise. When I reached the bare bone, I was as much myself as I had ever been.

And then he hunted down a new face for me so that he could begin the process all over again. That's the simple truth.

I know people will find this hard to believe after my conviction. I want everyone to know, my fans, my friends and family, all those people who have kept faith with me over the years, that we are in the process of preparing an appeal that I am confident will be successful. To my supporters, I say, Wait. Your faith will be justified. My innocence will be proven. To my enemies I say, You will not prevail over us.

Sara is a sweet child and it is a matter of intense sorrow – no, pain – no, *heartbreak* – to me that she was so cruelly treated while in my care. I trusted Dr Kaye. He was more than my physician, he was my friend. He abused that position. But what he did, he did without my permission or knowledge. If I had known – if I'd only known – I would have killed him with my own bare hands rather than allow him to do what he must have been planning all along. I have no doubt he did it solely in order to regain his reputation. I believe that everything he did was with that aim in mind. I repeat, I had no knowledge of any of it.

Remember that Sara was not this man's only victim. He abused me, too. My abuse was not sudden like Sara's. It took place over many years but the end result was the same – he took away my face. People say that there's a difference: he did it with my permission. Well, I plead guilty to being a fool, to being gullible, to being full of hope and believing in people more than I should have. I plead guilty to hoping to be well, to hoping for a normal life, to wanting to be able to look in the mirror without being disgusted by what I see. I have no explanation as to why I allowed such a monster to talk me into giving away something I valued so very much. Our faces are so much more than just appearance. When he took my face away from me, Dr Kaye also took away my soul to serve his greed for knowledge. Foolishly, I agreed to it, but I am no less a victim for that.

No one will ever stroke my cheek, no one will ever kiss me. He turned me into a freak and I will never forgive him for that, any more than I will forgive him for what he did to Sara.

I'd also like to say something about certain rumours that have been circulating in the press. There never were any other girls. Sara saw things, I understand that and believe it, but that is not proof. What those visions were and what they mean, I am only now just beginning to discover. One day, when I know more myself, I may be willing to share that information but in the meantime my lips must remain sealed. At one point during her stay Sara came to me with a photograph of one of our previous employees, a girl who used to keep house for me. Her name, I believe, was Catherine Monroe. Katie had left us some years before. So far we have been unable to trace her movements, but we have leads and I am hoping to be able to produce her to clear those rumours up once and for all. If she is out there, listening – Katie, I beg you to come forward and help put an end to these malicious stories my enemies are spreading about.

I appeal to you and to all my millions of fans for any information, any lead, no matter how small, that might help us track Katie down.

Finally, I want to thank my fans for keeping faith with me. My promise to you all is that your faith is not unjustified. Meanwhile, we have set up a charitable foundation to help people with similar sorts of problems to Sara and myself, called the Sara Carter Jonathon Heat Foundation. Anyone who wants to help should put their efforts towards the foundation, or make donations.

> Thank you all.
> See you soon.
> Jonathon Heat

Hiding from the House

When the security system crashed, taking with it all the power in the house, Tom Woods predictably blamed Mark for messing things up and Heat, who was furious at the blackout, quickly agreed that he should be kept away from the control room from now on. So Woods got his way in the end. And he was right; it was Mark's fault, but not because he'd messed up, fooling around with something he didn't understand. Mark had engineered his sweet minutes in the cupboard with Sara by programming the blackout himself.

He didn't mind being banned from the computer. It no longer mattered. He'd already wi-fied himself into the mainframe via his laptop and Palm Pilot. He could now control the entire house from the comfort of his bedroom without Tom or anyone else there knowing anything about it. He hadn't even had to visit the control room to arrange the blackout – he'd done it from his Palm Pilot in a cubicle in the toilets. It had taken all of five minutes.

'It wasn't that I was, like, this big genius,' Mark told me later on. 'It was just that Woods was, like, this big idiot.

I don't know why Heat was employing him; he was so far out of his depth. He was still trying to flick switches. That system was like a ghost – you could practically walk through walls with it, and he just had it sitting in a corner staring at them.'

Now that he had touched her again, Mark had it bad. For the next few days, Sara was all he could think about. Every time he thought of those illicit kisses in the dark, he felt dizzy with lust. He wanted to dance with her all right – horizontally. He had to see her again, and he had the means to do it. Next time, he would be more subtle. He didn't want to alert Heat and Woods to what he was doing by strangling the whole system whenever he wanted to see her. Sooner or later they'd call in a real expert who'd very quickly spot what he was up to. He wanted to be able to go where he wanted without anyone knowing anything about it, leaving no traces or tracks behind him.

He spent the next days trying to 'haunt' the house, as he called it – devising a stealth program that would allow him to move through it without the system noticing him. Basically, he was going to make the house look the other way. That was far more difficult than just crashing it, and it took a lot longer than ten minutes. To make matters worse, Heat had not only exiled Mark from the security room – he had exiled him from the house itself. Perhaps he suspected where Sara was during the blackout. Mark now slept in a gatehouse. His new job was letting cars in and out of the main gates during the day and patrolling the perimeter fence in the evenings – both jobs that kept him out of wireless reach of the mainframe. He was only able to connect at night, by creeping close to the house and sitting under a window while he worked. There he sat, shivering in the cold dark for hour after hour, worming his way into the mainframe and, camera by camera, through the house.

It took him a week of hard work to get his system up and running – a week of great anxiety because every day he left it was another day for Sara to forget him. But at last it was done. Now he had complete control over Heat's electrical and security systems.

'You have no secrets from me now,' Mark whispered to the house. He had set up a loop on the cameras, one by one, so that he could override them and put them on play, record or simply freeze them whenever he wanted to. It was scary. In a strange way, he felt as if the house was Jonathon Heat himself and the mainframe was his heart and mind; and the heart and mind of Jonathon Heat were places he really didn't want to go.

Eight days after the party, Mark was ready to make his move.

It was a bad business. It was all very well having control of the system, but he had no control of the guards who paced the house at night. He could check the corridors out on the Palm Pilot before he stepped into them – he could see through the cameras as well – but the Palm Pilot was small and it didn't respond as quickly as he would have liked. If they caught him, he'd be out, and his kisses with Sara at an end. If they discovered the security codes for the whole house on his Palm Pilot, he wouldn't just be hitting the road, he'd be hitting the court – with some force, if all the stories about Heat's lawyers were true. As we've seen since, they most certainly were. Mark was also anxious about how Sara would react. They'd exchanged texts, she'd said she wanted to see him again, and on the strength of this he'd decided to take her by surprise. All she knew was he had a plan. It had seemed like a good idea at the time, but, come the night, he was unsure. Maybe she'd only gone with him that night because she was angry with Heat for not letting her in on his performance. What if she regretted it and was only saying she wanted to see him again because she thought he couldn't? Creeping through the house at midnight, all these things felt far too real to Mark.

The house had many eyes, but not much brain. People are the other way round. Mark stole along the corridors, pausing at each corner and before each door, checking on the little screen of the Palm Pilot to see if anyone was there – not easy on such a small screen – before freezing the camera for a few minutes, so that he could carry on his way without being spotted.

Up to the foot of the big stairs – far too dangerous; so many corridors and doors led on to the stairway, and the lifts were like traps. Instead he snuck up the back stairs. Along more corridors, past more doors, all ready to open, all full of security men for all he knew – until, at last, he got to her door. He stood a minute, thinking, What am I waiting for? So he didn't. He knocked.

As usual, Sara had spent the day with Heat. They'd been shopping in the morning, had lunch at Heathcote's and then dropped by on a recording studio to listen to some takes he'd had done a few days earlier. They came to and left the studio by the back entrance in an effort to escape publicity, but someone had tipped off the paps. Wearing her mask, no one could know who Sara was, and so they'd posed for them, mouth to mouth in their masks. Again, Heat had slipped his tongue through into her mouth, not so briefly this time. Sara waited patiently while he licked the inside of her lips.

To Sara, it was the price of fame and fortune. Sleeping with Heat would be a kind of sacrifice, a rite, a ceremony. It would become part of her myth, that she and he had been lovers. She didn't mind – a part of her wanted to. As a man, Heat was unpleasant, but as a star, he was very sexy indeed. He had slept with hundreds or maybe even thousands of women before. He moved like no one on earth; he was desired by millions. All this was exciting, but, even so, Sara took the view that the later it happened the fewer times she'd have to do it. With her, all things sexual brought her thoughts back to Mark. He was her sexual voice. She could not have such a relationship with him in Heat's house, or so she believed, but all the time she was aware of an invisible connection between them, a bond of desire, heart to heart, chest to chest, sex to sex. Almost every night, she remembered making love to him. Since those lovely few minutes in the cupboard, she had been thinking about him all the time. So that night, when she opened the door to a knock and saw him standing there, she actually yelped with surprise and excitement.

Her face was a picture. Afterwards, Mark remembered it like an X-ray, because she was wearing her mask and all he actually saw was her jaw drop and her eyes flash; but even so he had a powerful image of her whole face going shock horror wow!

She glanced left and right, then stared stricken at the camera watching her over his shoulder. Mark was cruel enough to wait just a second while she fumbled for words before he held up his Palm Pilot proudly.

'I blinded the house. It can't see a thing.'

Sara stared from him, to the camera, to the Palm Pilot.

'Blinded,' he said again. 'They can't see us.' Then he added, 'Can I come in?'

Sara stepped to one side to let him in and then closed the door behind him.

'You idiot,' she hissed. 'You're going to wreck everything.'

'I blinded it,' he repeated, holding up his little machine. 'I control ze house. Nuzzink 'appens 'ere unless I say so.'

'What are you on about?'

'I can program the CCTV with this. I can program the whole fackin' house. I just freeze the cameras. They can't see a thing.'

Sara took a little bit of convincing, but once she believed him she was delighted.

'Wow. You bastard. The whole house? You can control the whole house?'

'I turned up the heating in Heat's room last night just to

make him sweat, baby.'

'So we can do what we want.'

It wasn't a question; it was a statement. Mark felt a familiar flicker of alarm. Sara! He'd been thinking he could get into her room and make love to her. She was thinking – what? That they could wander around the house stealing antiques or taking photos for *Heat* magazine or some other dangerous adventure. Well, of course she was – it was obvious. He was amazed at himself for not realising it before.

'Well, but what about the guards? I can't control the guards obviously. It's people that are dangerous. Ain't it always the case?' he said.

'You're James Bond,' she said. Despite himself, Mark grinned and pointed the Palm Pilot at her like a gun.

'Bang.'

His eyes drifted over to the bed, but Sara had already moved on.

'Thank God you turned up. I was going out of my mind with boredom. This place is like prison. But now! Now we can do what we like...!'

She turned to him and beamed. 'Hey,' she said. 'Let's go for a walk.'

All the way, Mark was having kittens. He'd been creeping about like a burglar, but Sara was strolling along, jabbering away like they were kids sneaking out to raid the fridge at midnight.

'It was all right for her,' he recalled. 'Heat wasn't going to send her anywhere. I was the one who'd get into trouble.'

At least she didn't want to go hunting around Heat's private apartments, as he'd feared; she wanted to go back down to the service area in the basement. Mark felt better once they were down there. The corridors upstairs were carpeted thickly, or laid with rugs, so that people could walk along in near silence. Down here, it was unfurnished, and bare, and you could hear people coming much better.

They found a room, empty except for a few chairs and tables stacked to one side. If Mark had worried before that she was using him to amuse herself, his doubts soon went. There was a bolt on the door and as soon as it was closed and locked, she turned to him for a kiss. Within moments they were both struggling to get out of their clothes, falling over their pants and getting their heads stuck in their tops in their efforts to get their hands on one another.

And then they made love.

Afterwards, Mark could easily have fallen asleep lying there with Sara wrapped around him, but she wanted to be up and doing. She pulled her clothes back together and wanted to explore.

'So you crashed the whole security system?' she asked.

'It's as blind as a bat,' boasted Mark.

She walked to the door and pushed it open.

Mark sighed, but he wanted to impress her too much to back down. He tapped in his codes on his Palm Pilot to test his control of the cameras outside, and the two went out to explore the house.

Eyes, yes, eyes everywhere in that house of secrets, peering down every corridor for shadows and unwanted visitors, for guests prying where they shouldn't go, looking across the floor for feet pattering, from the ceiling to examine the crown of your head. Down here there were as many as upstairs. Obviously, Heat wanted to keep tabs on his staff as much as his guests.

They walked in a cloak of invisibility, blinding each eye with what it had seen a minute or two before as they came towards it. Clever boy! Too clever, perhaps, for his own good. As he walked he kept glancing to the girl at his side. Her face was bare now. Bare was how he loved her. After seeing her about the house and in magazines and on websites wearing her mask, he found her naked face incredibly erotic. Her skin was like golden silk. What on earth was she doing in this ogre's den?

You'd have thought that a place with so many eyes must be full of secrets, but they found nothing. It was all empty corridors down there, rooms full of equipment, old stage props, abandoned furniture and other cast-offs. There was a recording studio, unused – Heat had another one upstairs in more congenial surroundings. The main control rooms, where Tom Woods and his staff controlled the house, were located further back. But at last, behind a set of double doors, they found another corridor, a long, straight passage with doors on each side. One of the fabled secret passages, perhaps, leading to who knows where? Sara and Mark went along it, opening each door one at a time and looking in, hoping to find some dark secret of Heat's tucked away down here. But it was the same story. The rooms were empty.

They found nothing different until they came to the last one.

As Sara approached that last door, ready to put out her hand to grasp the handle, something changed. Something about the door... She paused and looked closely at it and saw that the surface of the door wasn't real. She let out a little cry of surprise. In fact, the door was dissolving in front of her eyes – or was it growing? She couldn't make it out for a moment, until she realised that she was actually watching something pass through the solid wood and move towards her. It was the apparition she had seen before, but this time it was right in front of her. Instinctively, she lifted her mask up to her face to protect herself.

The creature was half free of the wood by now. This close she could see why it had no face; the face had been removed. She could see the marks of the knife round the sides where it had been neatly sliced off and pulled away. Instead of features, there was just this terrible wound, a blood-smeared death's-head. But what made it even more terrible was the fact that the eyes were still intact. So close, Sara could see into them quite clearly. They were deep, soft, velvety blue eyes. Kind eyes. In that desert of bone and blood, they seemed horribly out of place – alive and seeing, thinking and feeling in the face of death.

Once again, the creature was wearing Sara's clothes. And once again, even though there was no face to see, she knew she had seen this person before; but where, she had no idea.

The apparition left the door. As it approached her, the temperature dropped.

Sara flung herself against the wall as the creature swerved to go around her and carried on up the corridor behind them, leaving behind it a smell of antiseptic and hot blood. It moved at a walking pace along the corridor until it turned the corner and disappeared. Sara dropped the mask and looked up at Mark, panting with fear and excitement. He was looking at her with an expression of anxious curiosity, and she realised at once that the apparition had been there for her eyes alone. Only she was witness to its existence. It had been so horribly real! And yet Mark had seen nothing...

'I...thought I saw something,' she said, unwilling to admit to what had just happened. She put her mask back on, trying to hide the emotions that were running through her.

'What's wrong? Are you all right?' demanded Mark, grabbing her arm. All he had seen was her cry out and fling herself to the wall, as if something was there when nothing was. She was making no sense at all.

Sara shook him off, dashed forward, seized the handle to the door through which the monster had emerged, and pulled. Nothing budged; the door was locked tight. She let out a little groan of anger and frustration before recovering herself. She tugged a few more times before turning to Mark, pretending again. 'A locked door. Now what can that mean?' she exclaimed. Mark was staring behind, over his shoulder, still trying to work out what she had seen. He turned to look at her.

'That thing.' She nodded down the corridor. 'Didn't you see it? A ghost or something, I dunno,' she said. She felt embarrassed by her vision, and had no idea what it meant or how to explain it to him. She shrugged.

'You just saw a ghost?'

She shrugged again. 'I thought I did, anyway,' she said, as if she was owning up. 'You know. Kinda.' She giggled and nodded behind her at the door. 'So what's that about?' she asked as casually as she could.

Mark glanced behind him again. A ghost seemed to him more important than a locked door, but to Sara, even though the vision had been as solid as the two legs she stood upon, it was the door that held the secret. She knew that at once, without knowing why. He began to tap into his Palm Pilot, trying to examine the area while Sara leaned with her back against the door, watching him and glancing over his shoulder to where the apparition had disappeared. Behind her, she felt the door begin to chill. Its temperature was dropping like a stone. Something must be drawing near.

'But there's no cameras here,' he said. Unlike everywhere else in the house so far, the corridor they were in was not mapped on the security system. For some reason, Heat had chosen to be blind there himself. There was something here he did not want to see, or be seen ...

Or, perhaps, he had simply never bothered. Or else they had never had the system put in here, so far away from anything of significance.

'If it's a secret, I want to see it,' said Sara. She stood upright. The door, which had a moment before felt like a block of ice, was now growing hot.

'Especially other people's,' said Mark, with a half-smile.

'Especially Heat's,' said Sara. 'I think he's up to something, don't you? Or if it's just an empty place, it could be our place,' she added, trying a touch of temptation.

They examined the door; there was a keyhole. They looked through it into darkness. Sara put on her mask, got down on her knees and sniffed around the door like a dog to smell what was inside. She stood up suddenly with an exclamation of disgust. Mark got down after her and sniffed. There was the faint but unmistakable whiff of rotting meat.

'It smells of death,' whispered Sara.

Mark turned to look at her and then sniffed again.

'A mouse got trapped in there, maybe,' he suggested. 'A mouse? Down here, miles from anywhere?'

'There's windows,' said Mark. Many of the rooms down there had windows, facing a gully round the back of the house. A small living thing might have slipped in and got trapped. Sara shook her head.

'I want to see inside,' she said. 'Can you work it out?' 'Well, not tonight, anyway.'

There was nothing else to be done. They left, Mark with his hands stuffed into his jeans pockets, Sara with her hand on his arm. As they went, she glanced behind her and saw under the door a faint light, through which shadows passed, as if someone inside were walking up to the door. The light flashed twice, then died.

'Strange, innit?' she asked Mark.

He pulled a face. 'It's just a locked door,' he said.

He walked her back to her room. Sara did not say any more to him that night about what she had seen. She stood on her tiptoes, kissed him on the mouth and fled to the safety of her bed. Mark left through the window he'd come in by and walked home alone across the wet fields. At home, he fell into bed and went to sleep at once.

Sara — 8 June 2005

(Sara is on her bed with the curtains drawn and a little light on. She is white and scared. She keeps peeping outside the curtains.)

OK. This is a record. I'm making a record of what happens. She's out there somewhere. She could be on the other side of the curtains right now. Outside, watching for me...

(Pause. She listens intently, but we hear nothing.)

Mark came tonight. I was so happy. I'd been thinking about him all week. And now this. What does it mean? She had no face and she's wearing my clothes. What does she want?

(She leans forward and whispers even more quietly.)

I've seen her before. Here. In this house, I know it! In a photograph. No, don't ask me how, she has no face. But she used to live here, I know it. I'm certain of it... One of the staff maybe.

What does she want? Wandering up and down the corridors at night, lost. And only for me! No one else sees her. Please, please, don't let me be going mad. But I'm not mad. You may think I am but I'm not. It means something. Everything means something. I just have to know what it is...

Or to warn me. Could be that. Could be.

I'll tell you this, if they did anything to that girl, I'll make sure they pay for it. Murder? Could be. That's what ghosts are sometimes here for, isn't it? I signed a donor card. Jonathon asked me to, he said he'd done it, it was only right. The op's in about five weeks. That's how long I have, because one thing's for sure – I ain't gonna be here when the man comes for me with the big knife – no way! I'm out of here. Someone else can do me later on. But for now I just have to keep quiet while I find out what's going on. So long as they never find out that I know. Five weeks to find out what's behind that door...

(There's a noise outside. Sara jumps and shrieks. She pulls the curtains tight, then peers out. She begins to shake and cry.)

Please leave me alone. Please go away. I'll do what I can. Please...

(She pulls the curtains, reaches up and rests her hand on the light switch. She peers at the crack between them.)

Are you afraid of the dark, too? But it's night-time.

(She turns out the light. There's a period of silence.) Can't we be friends? *(There's a rattle as she turns the camera off.)*

Who's That Girl?

Mark had no idea what visions Sara had seen.

The word ghost on her lips didn't convince him. She'd often seen such things in the past and mostly they had a rational explanation. A UFO turned out to be an aeroplane emerging from behind the clouds, a ghost hovering in her bedroom transformed into the reflection from a streetlamp through a crooked window pane. A shadow cast by a concealed walker, the echo of a footfall from behind a building, light on water, the wind blowing over the soil-pipe – Sara was far too keen to turn the mysterious into the supernatural for Mark to take such things seriously. Even when her sightings remained unexplained, they were always presences half seen, half felt, and there was always the suspicion that there was an ordinary explanation somewhere if only it could be found.

This had been different – vivid, unmistakable, impervious to rationality. It had filled her senses and nearly overwhelmed her, but she had not let him know that.

Much later, when he had seen the video diary, Mark was amazed.

'She never let on. Later on, she got more anxious, but that night you'd never have guessed she'd seen anything like that.'

Yet there were hints. When he awoke the next morning, Mark found a text on his phone, sent at half past two the previous morning.

'Ghost outside curtain,' it read. 'What shall I do?'

That was all. When he texted her and asked about it, she replied, 'I told it stories.'

'What sort of stories?' he asked.

'Ghost stories, of course,' said Sara, and laughed.

The videos tell another tale, but there again, as Mark himself pointed out, it may be that the diaries themselves aren't real. Sara herself no longer speaks, but it may be that they're just another voice she invented to amuse herself and, perhaps, us. There again they may be true only in parts. Truth to Sara seems to have been just one more piece in the game she played with who and what she was. Nothing else she said or did can be taken at face value; there's no reason to treat those diaries as any different.

So far as Mark was concerned at that point, the significant thing about the evening was not the ghost or the locked door, but the fact that they had got together again. In the storeroom that night they had made love in the glare of the neon strips overhead, but afterwards Sara had found a little lamp and put that on instead. There in the gloom they admitted to each other at last that they were in love. Yes – the real thing. They had been together and they had been apart, and all they had been able to think about was the other one – being with them, talking to them, sharing with them,

133

making love to them. Even in the overarching presence of Jonathon Heat, Sara admitted that Mark had been there in the forefront of her mind.

'We should be together,' Mark had said.

'Soon, we'll be inseparable,' Sara replied.

Soon – but not yet. First, fame and fortune. Mark didn't want to spoil the night and he held his peace, but sooner rather than later, he would try to talk her out of her plans. Fame and fortune by all means – but not like this! Not through Jonathon Heat. And no surgery. Above all, please, no surgery with Dr Kaye. It wasn't really that he was scared she'd damage their sex life, although it did bother him. All his instincts, all he knew about her, were against it. Her inclination to hurt herself, her periodic bouts of self-destruction – the fact that this very doctor had been so abusive with those same problems in Heat – all these things rang every warning bell he had.

He had no illusions about how hard it was going to be. How do you talk someone out of their dreams when their dreams are only just coming true? So it was very much to his surprise when she offered a way out herself.

Later the next day, Mark rang her and found out more about the ghost – the faceless girl walking out of the door, the smell of antiseptic and blood, the fact that she was wearing Sara's clothes. Mark was put out that they had found love, made love, declared love – and then off she went seeing faceless monsters. But he put his pique to one side. He saw the meaning of it at once.

'It was wearing your clothes; it has no face, same as

Jonathon Heat has no face. It's walking his house. What else do you think it means?' he demanded. 'It's about you. It's about surgery. You're having your face done by his doctor. It's obvious!'

'She's not me,' said Sara. 'She's someone else.'

'She's wearing your clothes.'

'Anyone can wear another person's clothes.'

'Ghosts go about trying on other people's clothes?'

'Why not? Anyway, I know who it is . . .'

For some reason, this statement appalled Mark. 'Who?'

Sara hesitated. 'I've seen her. I don't know her name. Here, in this house. I think she must be one of the staff.'

Despite himself, Mark felt a thrill of fear and fascination. 'Is?' he repeated. 'Are you saying that this girl . . . she's still alive?'

'Maybe. I've seen her face. Or maybe it's a photo . . .'

'Oh, come on!'

'I'll prove it. I'll find her.' Sara nodded. 'Then we'll see.'

Mark had a sudden flash of memory – Jessica telling him the story about Sara shouting at the mirror . . . 'Who's that girl? Who's that girl? Get her out of my room . . .'

'Or the mirror,' he said. 'Maybe you saw her there.'

There was a long pause. 'Bollocks,' said Sara in a flat voice, and he knew he'd made her angry. Later, Mark was to regret not following up this line of thought with her, but at the time he decided that he'd been led away from his intention and made his way back to his argument. 'But that's not the point. So what if it's someone else? All that would mean is someone else has been fucked around before you.'

Not believing his own argument – he was just thinking on his feet – Mark hardly expected her to. But Sara agreed. 'Exactly!' she exclaimed. 'What, then? Maybe I'm not the first. How many has he had here? And, Mark – what does he want them for? What do you think? Why does he want young girls?'

Mark snorted in amusement. Why did a rock star want young girls? But that was obviously not the answer.

'Or why does he want young girls' faces?' said Sara. And now Mark felt the terrors run right through him, because Sara had seen a girl who had lost her face; and what was it in all the world that Jonathon Heat wanted most?

'That can't be true . . . no, that's ridiculous . . . surely . . .' he stuttered. She must be joking!

But Sara replied without amusement.

'I'll tell you what,' she said. 'I don't think I'm so keen any more on letting that old Dr Face Gobbler anywhere near me with his knives. But something's going on in this house. We have to find out what it is.'

'We?' squeaked Mark. But he knew it was true. They were in this together. He wasn't going to leave her now.

'I'll find the girl,' said Sara. 'You get us behind that door. Then we can talk about getting out of here before the op.'

This conversation terrified Mark. He had been so happy – for one night only. Now in the morning there were ghosts and Heat had turned into a monster – a murderer, a thief of faces, an abductor of young girls. Such a public man to have such a terrible private life! Dark missions had hatched during the night, objectives to be fulfilled, mysteries to be solved, terrible dangers to negotiate.

But what nonsense it all was! Heat was mad, but not that mad. Did Sara really believe he was plotting to steal her face? Mark put down the phone, lay down on his bed and wept.

But not for long. As always, his worry was for Sara. What had liberated these terrible thoughts and visions? Was it a real ghost? Or was it what he had always feared for her – creeping madness, and delusions of danger tearing her soul apart? On the other hand, what if she was seeing something real? Mark did not necessarily believe Sara, but he did believe in ghosts for the simple reason that he had seen the evidence. He had an aunt, his grandmother's sister, who knew the dead well. She attended a spiritualist church in Wythenshawe, where she lived with no human company, but not alone, as she always said: with her dead husband, Terry, her spirit guide, Missy Salome, and her pet cats and caged birds. Mark, along with his brothers and sisters, all thought she was mad until one day she showed him there was more to it.

As a child, he owned a tan-and-white mongrel terrier called Taylor, who was always escaping and running away from home. The dog's senses were so sharp he quivered with life, but he'd get so deeply involved in what he was doing that he'd forget where he was. He'd had two car accidents in this state, which led to a heavy limp in his right back leg and bad hearing. The end came when he was down the park pestering a horse – a brown filly, who was that much quicker and more nervous than the old gelding who had been there for years. The horse got fed up with Taylor yapping at her, waited until he was digging for rabbits in the hedge, walked up behind him and stamped on his head. Taylor quivered once more and then lay still.

Mark was at home at the time and ran like the wind when he heard. He cradled the cooling dog and raged against the horse, who stood watching him from the far side of the field. He took his pet home wrapped in a blanket and buried him like a Viking with all his favourite things in the hole with him – his current bone, his blanket, a scattering of Good Boy Chocs, a dried pig's ear and his collar and lead. The only thing missing was his ball, which had mysteriously disappeared.

A few days later, his aunt amazed him by telling him where it was. Taylor had run off with it on that last fatal journey and dropped it among the laurels to one side of the mansion house whose grounds the park had once been. Doubtfully, Mark went to have a look – and there it was. Joyfully he carried it back, plastic proof of a world beyond this one.

'How did you know?' he asked her.

'Taylor told me,' his aunt replied proudly. From then on Mark was a believer. He even snuck out against his mother's wishes to watch his aunt and other mediums performing in church, where he saw messages carried between the living and the dead on a weekly basis.

So the world of the dead was real to Mark, but the little proofs put forward in church were an entirely different thing from Sara's. They were friendly messages from homely spirits, family and neighbours who no longer happened to be visible.

This thing of Sara's with its torn-off face, its stink of blood and hospitals was altogether mad. Mark believed in spirits, but he believed in madness, too, and in hallucination. To his mind, it was far more likely that what Sara saw were her own thoughts and feelings animated in her eyes, rather than anything with a real life outside of her own.

Only one thing was clear, whether this was hallucination and delusion or all for real, Sara was suffering. She had to get out – she had to escape. If she wouldn't go of her own accord, he had to make her. But how to go about this was not so obvious.

His first thought, despite Sara's stories, and his own suspicions about Heat and Dr Kaye, was actually to go and tell them what she was thinking. He did not believe that Heat was as dangerous as she suddenly seemed to think – he thought of him more as a victim himself – and although Kaye was fatally flawed, Mark did not yet think that he had done any of this on purpose, certainly not that he would kill for body parts to carry out his plans. Kaye, he thought, was more wrong than bad and, if he knew that Sara was having thoughts like these, surely he'd call off the operation, for now at least.

But Sara would never forgive him. In the end, it was that thought rather than any belief in what she was saying that held him back. For the same reason he dismissed thoughts of telling her mother. Jessica was a known flake, she'd be bound to overreact somehow, come storming in and make a mess of things one way or the other. Jessica always caused more crises than she ever solved.

Another option was to follow Sara's plan and try to get to the other side of that door. The trouble with that was, if she was hallucinating, as Mark believed, opening the door wouldn't stop anything. She'd still be seeing ghosties and ghoulies and suffering delusions that there were dark secrets to be uncovered. She'd probably only put up another obstacle, another condition, and then another, until it was all too late. And if it was true . . . well, that was madness, sure, because what fool walks into the ogre's den? 'That's what we have police for,' said Mark to himself, although he knew very well there was no evidence that would get them to take on this job. And, anyway, what would happen if Heat caught them? Then Mark would be sent away and she would be left behind – his lovely Sara, surrounded by enemies and delusional fears, with only Heat's mad hand to hold.

It was a dilemma. Mark needed some advice. He rang up the only person he knew who knew Sara as well as he did – Janet.

The first thing she asked was, 'Have you spoken to Jessica about it?'

'No,' said Mark. 'Do you think I should?'

'Oh, no,' replied Janet. 'Don't do that. She'd make a mess somehow, you know what she's like.' She sat down on the edge of her bed and chewed her nail. The fact was, Sara had anticipated Mark by ringing Janet up the night before. They'd had their usual long rambling conversation and, along the way, Sara had dropped in her latest game with Mark – seeing ghosts. Janet remembered the apparition she'd been seeing in the corridors? Well, she'd made a whole story up about it just for Mark – as usual, just made it up on the spur of the moment, more to wind him up than anything else.

Janet was annoyed with her. She liked Mark, and she knew Sara had strong feelings for him. She'd seen how hurt she'd been when they'd split up. Part of the reason for the split in the first place had been Sara's silly games and here she was doing it all over again.

'Don't you think you're getting a bit old for that sort of thing?' she'd said.

'Ooh, get you.'

'I like him, that's all. And so do you. So why piss him around?'

Sara had been rather light about it. It wasn't a big deal, just a game. He was such a clever box, she wanted to see how clever he really was, if he could actually get behind that door. It was just a bit of fun... So she claimed.

'He's your boyfriend, Sara.'

'He deserves it for dumping me.'

'That's silly.'

'I suppose,' Sara sighed. 'I guess you're right. He'd be really hurt if he found out. I'll get out of it, don't worry. But don't tell him, whatever you do. I'll get out of it somehow, OK?'

Now, listening to Mark worrying to her over the phone, Janet was more annoyed with her than ever. Sara was unwise – but she was also her oldest and best friend, and loyalty stopped her from telling him what was going on. It wasn't the sort of thing you interfered with. It was up to Sara to get out of it. But Janet resented being made a part of such games, and was touched by how worried Mark was about her friend.

'She hasn't said anything to you?' asked Mark.

'No,' lied Janet obediently.

'What do you think?' he asked.

'Oh, just go along with it for now, see what happens. It'll probably all sort itself out without you having to do anything,' she said vaguely. 'She'll forget about it in a day or two. You know her.'

Mark thought about it. 'She's really putting a lot of pressure on me to get behind that door, that's the thing,' he said.

'See if it lasts,' insisted Janet. 'She'll probably have forgotten all about it by tomorrow. It'll blow over. just… don't do anything for now and see what happens.'

They didn't talk for long – Janet felt too uncomfortable about the deception for that. Mark did mention Sara's second thoughts about surgery at Home Manor Farm, but Janet, her mind on her lie, didn't make much of it – only that it would probably be better if Sara didn't go ahead with it.

She didn't want to leave Mark with nothing and so, before she put the phone down, she told him that she believed Sara loved him.

'That's good,' he said. 'Cos you know what? I think I might love her, even.'

Janet's heart cracked.

'You don't think she might be making all this up, do you?' she asked cautiously.

'Do you think so?' asked Mark.

'You know what she's like.'

'Bitch, if she is!'

'But you know Sara, she just goes spinning off and then she can't get out of it; it's just the way her mind works,' said Janet, trying to redeem her friend. 'Or maybe she makes bits of it up. I sometimes wonder if she really knows what the truth is.'

'That's what scares me,' said Mark.

He put the phone down disconsolately. Janet's advice was good. Sara would most likely forget all about the ghost and getting behind the door within a week at the latest. But he hadn't discovered anything that would help him get her out of Home Manor Farm. At least she had agreed in principle. The only thing now, it seemed, was to wait for the ghost to blow over and try to talk Sara into leaving sooner rather than later. But he knew he had the whole power of Jonathon Heat, his wealth, his fame, his people and his vision, working against him. How could one young man with a dodgy Palm Pilot work against that?

The answer, he told himself, was with his heart full of love. Oh, yes – Mark was, and is, a romantic. And maybe he was vain enough to believe that he could be a hero.

Ghostly visions, lies and deception, silly games, fame, boundless ambition and an imagination that could transform ordinary things into pure magic – no wonder Sara comes down to us as such a tangle of contradictions. What did she really see, what did she really think – what were her hopes and aims? We only have the clues she left behind to work it out.

Concerning her visions, we have three elements of evidence – her video diary, what she told Mark and what she told Janet. Which was true we do not know. Janet certainly believed that up until then Sara had never tried any of her games and imaginings on her – she always told her what was real and what wasn't. On this occasion, she's not so sure.

'I wonder if she was just protecting me. If she knew how dangerous things really were in that place, she had reason to keep me away.'

Perhaps. Either way, Sara had neutralised the concern of her best friend by telling her that the ghosts were games played on Mark. When Janet rang her up later that same night, she asked her about something else Mark had said that Sara had not mentioned the night before – that she was having second thoughts about the surgery. When this was confirmed Janet was delighted. She, too, thought Sara was mad to have any changes made, except perhaps to the burn mark on her face. Now that Sara said she was thinking of saying no, she realised how relieved she was.

'But don't string it out too long,' she said. 'It's not really fair on Jonathon, is it? Or Dr Kaye.'

'Not fair on Dr Kaye, no,' replied Sara. 'I'll be quick.'

'And let poor old Mark off the hook. He was petrified for you.'

'I promise,' said Sara. And then they both got the giggles.

Falling in Love Again

Mark had a pretty good idea about where to look for the key to that door, if he wanted to. Tom Woods always wore a vast bunch of keys on his belt and Mark had often wondered what on earth they were for. The man had a state-of-the-art security system at his fingertips, every important door in the house had an electronic key – why did he need to carry half a kilo of metal around all day long? If they were just duplicates for the bedrooms and suchlike, he hardly needed them on his person.

In fact, Woods liked the weight of a good heavy bunch of keys on his belt – it made him feel more in charge, somehow. Most of the keys on the bunch didn't even have a lock to fit. They were security keys for the security man. Mark had spent enough time in the security room to know that there were no duplicates kept there. That bunch was definitely the place to look, but, as far as Mark could see, Woods carried the keys at all times. That meant he had to get into Woods's apartment and hunt around while he slept. Rummaging about in Woods's trousers while the man snored and groaned in bed next to him, ready to wake at any moment – Woods often boasted that being a light sleeper was an essential trick for every security guard – was not his idea of fun. It could be done...

But not quite yet. A few days later, Mark made his way up to Sara's room to discuss leaving the house, ghosts, locked doors, murder, mayhem and surgery. Instead, they made love. Much better than rooting about through Tom Woods's trousers. Much nicer than sneaking about Heat's state-of-the-art house, trying to uncover secrets that probably weren't even there in the first place. No competition.

Sara fully intended to get behind that door, but the ghost scared her so much, she was happy to let it ride. Instead, they closed the curtains on the four-poster bed, drank beer, watched TV, made love, had long conversations about fame, art, life and sex, and developed deep, dark bags under their eyes through living double lives – one by day and one by night. Mark did his best to convince her to leave anyway. He'd presented his arguments against surgery many times before, but now, to his surprise and delight, she seemed to be willing to listen. He railed against the whole concept of surgical youth. He hated the way people wiped life away from themselves – their hard-won crow's-feet, their smile lines, their sad furrows cut away by the surgeon's knife. The celebrity mothers who had their silicone implants removed early in pregnancy to prevent stretching, then had their babies by Caesarean at eight months before they got big, followed by liposuction on their bums and thighs and a full stomach tuck to take up the loose skin; the rock stars who changed their noses and chin lines every few years; the old women who looked at the world with ancient eyes out of the faces of girls; the old men who forced their middle-aged bodies into young skins – he despised them all. What's wrong with growing old? Your wrinkles when they come, your loose skin, were signs of a life lived, they should be worn with pride. Jonathon Heat, Michael Jackson, Cher – they all looked ridiculous, turning themselves into dolls, some of them disasters, some more successful, but all awful, all ugly – all wrong. They were not themselves any more, and what are you, if not yourself? And, despite all their efforts and their fabulous wealth, they'd grow old and die anyway. If you fight life, you will lose . . .

Above all, he told her, he couldn't understand why she, who was about as beautiful as it was possible to get, should want to change anything about herself. Mark's words brought tears to his own eyes, because, to him, Sara was beautiful as the day. He swore to her, if she could see herself as he saw her, she'd never change a single thing.

Sara lay in his arms, smiling as if this was all she needed to hear. Mark grew passionate; he wanted more than anything for Sara to leave this mad house and this mad desire for a new face, and go back into the ordinary world.

He bent down and touched her mouth. 'Don't do it,' he said. 'I can't bear the idea of this face I've just kissed being anyone except you. And Heat! He's a joke, a doll, something made up, not real at all – not like you.'

Sara laughed with delight. She had been called a lot of things but never real before now.

'Beauty is more than skin deep,' she joked. 'Or do you only like me for my looks?'

'Your face goes all the way to your heart,' said Mark, surprising both of them with his eloquence. He bent down and kissed the red triangular scar across her jaw.

They had two lovely weeks. During the day, Sara went shopping, took lessons in singing and dancing, modelled, accompanied Heat everywhere. At night she forgot her ambitions in Mark's arms. Two lovely weeks; and then she had another visitation.

It came to her in her room. Once before it had visited her there, but then it had been a sense, a presence; this time it appeared in its full glory.

She was woken out of a deep sleep by a sudden scream, so violent and so close that it had her trying to run through the wall behind her, heart in her mouth, before she knew she was awake. She could see nothing, but she knew exactly where it was – standing just on the other side of the curtains drawn round the bed. It was so close she could see its breath stirring the fabric. As she leapt up from sleep, there was a pause, but a second later it began again. The ghost – the girl – was screaming and begging for something – mercy, or death, perhaps. Her voice was so badly scrambled that it was almost impossible to make anything out, except that she was in the most atrocious pain. Sara pushed herself right up against the back of the bed, unable to move her eyes from the place where the demonic screaming was coming from, less than a breath away from the curtains, unable to move or even to breathe. Then, as if in answer to an unspoken question, the curtains dissolved from her eyes – and there she stood, howling like a dog almost, her bony jaws opening and closing like death aping life.

'Help me,' begged the figure, the words distorted by the fact that she had no lips. Then the words disintegrated into an agony of screams and sobs again.

The vision was so real that at first Sara was convinced that it was actually flesh and blood. The whole face was a skull, and now she could see clearly that an all-too human hand had done it. The blood vessels were neatly sutured and tied off, the nerves held in little plastic tubes, ready for reconnection.

Suddenly, Sara found herself again and rushed forward to try and comfort the poor girl, who was a monster after all only in her agony. But as her hands reached out in comfort, they passed straight through the body. She stared, stunned by what had happened. She lifted her hands to her face to see, and saw that they were smeared with blood. She screamed herself – huge, helpless screams of pure terror and disgust that hurt her throat.

The creature turned from Sara – she had an impression of hope on her face, even though she didn't have one – staggered across to the door and then straight through it. Sara, whose heart felt as if it was going to burst with fear, pity and disgust, turned on her bedside lamp, and realised in the second that the light clicked on that even though she had seen the ghost standing at the foot of the bed, even though she had watched it turn and drift through her door, the curtains to the four-poster had been drawn the whole time. Now, those same curtains were like a shield hiding her, because she had the courage neither to draw them and see, nor to keep them closed, for fear of what they hid. The stench of blood was still thick on her tongue and it was a full minute before she was able to press her finger down on the button that opened the curtains, convinced that the second she did, that terrible blood-soaked face would be thrust at her through the fabric. But when she peeped through there was nothing to be seen except a patch of something wet on the carpet, which faded as she reached down and was dry by the time she touched it.

It was another five minutes before she was able to get out of bed and open her bedroom door to see if there was any sign of the girl in her corridor. This time, she took her video camera with her.

Sara — 23 June 2005

(The camera is trembling violently and Sara is making choked sobbing noises — desperately trying to stay quiet but unable to control her breathing. The camera flicks over the floor in her room. Then we see the door open and get a view down the corridor)

Oh my God, oh God! Look — it's blood. Oh Jesus, it was real, it was real . . . Look! Look! Shit. God, I'm so scared. Blood. It stinks! She was real . . .

(The camera is pointing to a red smear on the wall. It looks as if someone has taken a blood-soaked rag and rubbed it against the wall as they walked past. The blood is trickling down the wall. Sara has started to pant.)

I just hope . . . I just hope she's dead. I just hope she's really a ghost. Please God, don't let her be alive, I couldn't bear it if she was alive. Looking like that! Imagine looking like that . . . Shit! Look — look!

(The camera lifts up from the wall and down the corridor, where we see a figure standing in the darkness. It waits for a second; all we can hear is Sara's ragged breathing. The camera is shaking violently, sometimes losing the image altogether. The figure waits for a few seconds, then the head twitches and we hear a distant but frantic screaming, broken up as if by a bad recording. The figure begins to move towards us.)

God, no!

(She runs back into her room, the camera taking a whirling chaos of images – the floor, Sara's feet, the figure behind, the blood on the wall and more on the carpet as she runs. The door slams behind her and she runs straight to her bed, panting and quivering and sobbing in the low light. She reaches across and turns the camera off.)

(The camera comes on again. It is focused on a group photograph on the wall. It is evidently some time later. Sara is calm.)

That's her. There. That's her. I found her.

(The camera zooms in shakily, closer and closer finding a face. We see a plump young woman, with a broad face, standing slightly sideways and smiling out of the picture at us. There is no way of linking her to the figure we briefly saw in the corridor. Sara has drawn a red line in felt tip round her to pick her out. The camera gets as close as it can, but it is shaking badly and we can't really make out much.)

There. Poor girl! I hope she's dead, that's all.

(She fiddles with the camera. Darkness.)

The Locked Door

Two days later, Mark was fiddling around in Tom Woods's trousers. Tom Woods himself wasn't in them, but he lay only a couple of metres away, heaving in his sleep. It was not Mark's thing at all. If he was caught, he'd be in police custody within an hour. And Sara would be on her own.

It was vile. Fear communicates. Mark had seen Sara in some states before, but never anything to compare with her terror the night after the apparition had found its way into her room. She rang him weeping, begging him to come to her. Mark did, working his way through the house to her room, where he found her trembling from head to foot, her nerves utterly shot, clinging to him and begging him to help her. Mark wanted to leave the house at once, but she refused. The vision was revealing itself to her for a reason. She was certain Kaye and Heat were behind it. The girl had lived here, hadn't she? She was one of the staff. She would go – after this only a fool would stay. But first they had to see behind that all-important door.

Mark made his deal. Right now Sara was waiting in her room, bag packed, ready to go. Once they had seen behind the door, they were off.

Mark fumbled in the dark, his hands shaking. Woods had the ring clipped onto a loop on his trousers and Mark couldn't figure out how to undo it in the dark. He almost cut it off. Why not? In an hour they'd be gone. But then he'd have shown his hand... So he struggled for minutes on end, it seemed, until finally he found the catch, slipped the keys quietly off and made his way upstairs to meet Sara.

Together, they walked down the long slope that led to the service area. Mark pressed the keys on his Palm Pilot that would close and open the cameras as they walked along, always looking over his shoulder, convinced that Dr Kaye and Jonathon Heat would suddenly appear out of the walls behind them. Sara hung on to his arm and looked ahead – her terrors were before her. She didn't want to scare him, but he knew very well what the little jumps and gasps she was making meant: the visions had begun again. Her progress down the corridor was marked with a series of pops and bangs, flashes of light and changes of temperature. As they got closer, she could hear someone hissing at her. Then, a dark male voice called her name, and she leapt into the air.

'What is it?' hissed Mark.

'Nothing – noises. C-can't you hear?' she stammered.

Mark shook his head. The night was still to him. All this was for her alone.

They approached the door. Now she could smell it – blood on the air, and the smell of decay. She had to force herself not to cringe as they drew near, terrified that the apparition would come rushing out of the wood straight at her. But then, when they got there, the noises stopped abruptly as if they knew she was there.

Sara got down on all fours and sniffed like a dog. Mark watched her bum in the air, lusted, and was afraid for her.

'Death, you see?' she exclaimed triumphantly. 'Something is dead in there.'

He got down himself and sniffed, but this time he detected nothing. On the other hand, he had a blocked nose. Sara heaved a sigh. Please God it wasn't going to happen again! She sat down with her back to the door and tried to relax, watching as Mark took off his bag and got out the keys, which he had wrapped up in a T-shirt to stop any noise.

Mark glanced at the keyhole and then at the keys, trying to sort out where to start. As he did so, the noises began again. They began with a soft pop; then, from the slight gap under the door, there was a flash of light.

Sara started fearfully and looked up at Mark, but it was obvious once again that he had no idea what was happening. He was looking down at her with a little frown on his face, as if he was waiting for an explanation of her behaviour. Sara grinned at him, both embarrassed and scared. To hide her fear she began to talk, jabbery gabble about what they were going to do when they left this place, how their lives would be together, safe happy lives. As she spoke, the noises increased – fizzes and pops and bangs, shadows, flashes and dull voices, bangs and thumps coming from the other side of the door. She conceived a terror that whatever it was behind there was about to seize her and drag her under the gap, squashing her to pulp in the process. Somehow, she knew that whatever it was was possessed of a truly demonic strength. And yet, out of sheer stubbornness, or embarrassment, or perhaps in an effort to prove to herself that it wasn't really there and had no power at all, she didn't move.

To Mark she seemed to be going mad. She was sitting there, holding her bottom off the ground with tension, gabbling nonsense, all the time making little starts and jumps, glancing from side to side, gasping excitedly, twitching and throwing herself from side to side. Suddenly, without warning, she literally jumped up from the ground and landed in Mark's arms.

'Can't you hear it?' she gasped. There had been a terrifically loud bang and a roar, the kind of noise a lion or a film monster might make, so loud, she thought it was literally about to break the door down and snatch her away.

'Hear what? There's nothing happening,' he hissed. She was really scaring him.

'But it's— Oh my God, can't you hear?' There was another huge bang, a bellow as if the Minotaur himself was coming, and then a man's voice speaking urgently but low, the words too blurred to make out. Then there came the sound of a girl suddenly screaming in pain. It was truly dreadful, a cawing, screeching noise, that she understood was coming from a pretty young throat.

Mark pushed her out of the way. He fitted one of the keys to the lock, then another.

'We'll see now,' he said grimly. Sara backed off, glancing over her shoulder – surely the noise was waking the whole house! – and watched as Mark began to go through the bundle of keys one after the other, trying to find one to fit.

Suddenly, the screaming stopped. Sara was aware of their own ragged breathing. The only noise was the low hum of the sleeping building and the sound of the keys rattling as Mark went through them. He went through the whole ring, maybe thirty keys, but he found nothing. Glancing at Sara, he paused. She had gone as white as a sheet.

'What's happening?' he begged.

'She's stopped. Maybe she's dead. Do you think they've killed her?'

Mark pulled a face. How could he know anything?

'Either I'm going mad or they killed someone in there. Just get it open.'

Mark licked his lips and turned to go through the keys again. This time, about a quarter of the way through, the lock turned.

He stood, tugged down the handle and the door swung open. And inside they saw – another door. There were a couple of metres of wall and then another door, a solid metal one this time. There was no keyhole.

Sara gave a low moan and flung herself at it. Her hands slid over the surface but there was no handle. She got down again to sniff, and her fingers, as she bent to support her weight, found something cold and strange under her palm. She lifted it up. It was the corner of a mouldy old sandwich that someone had dropped days ago and then forgotten about.

Sara dropped it as soon as she realised what it was. It stank of decay. Mark crouched down on his knees and opened it up with the end of a key.

'Sausage,' he said.

He looked up, their eyes met. There was a pause. Then they both had a sudden attack of the giggles.

For a moment they couldn't look at each other, trying desperately to keep quiet. The sandwich was hilarious. Mark had a joke he wanted to get out about the sausage ghost, and not being able to speak was just making him worse. But the amusement didn't last long. Suddenly, Sara let out a shout of fright. Mark followed her gaze to the metal door. He saw nothing, but in front of her, only inches away, a figure began to slowly emerge: the girl with no face.

She was bleeding again but this time made no noise as she walked almost majestically out of the door, which seemed to bulge and then melt back into shape as she passed through it. Sara had to press herself into the wall to give her space to pass, but, even so, the figure brushed against her as it went. In front of the second door, which they had closed to stifle their noise, the monster stopped and waited, as if it couldn't pass. Sara glanced into her face, and saw the gory terror – the arched teeth with no lips, the bleeding bone all bare of flesh except for two wide, clear eyes that returned her look with a curious gaze.

Sara groaned and retched. She pressed herself to the wall, closed her eyes and turned her face away, gesturing Mark to look. Mark glanced over his shoulder but he saw nothing. He touched her lightly on the arm. Sara looked up. The ghost was still there, waiting patiently for God knows what.

'Open the door for her,' groaned Sara, and watched in horror as Mark leaned right through the tormented figure and turned the handle. At once, the girl carried on her way. Sara ran out after her, but within two steps the apparition had disappeared. Only a faint smell of blood and antiseptic on the air remained.

Sara stopped, feeling helpless and useless before such pain. She turned to look at Mark, standing behind watching her, and began to weep.

Mark took her in his arms. 'Now we go,' he said.

She shook her head.

'I opened it, didn't I?' demanded Mark furiously.

'That's not the point,' she replied.

Mark turned to examine the second door.

'There's no way in,' he said.

Sara said nothing, but stared over his shoulder at the plain metal surface. Faintly, behind it, the screaming was beginning again. And this time, very faintly indeed, Mark could hear it, too.

Later, back in her room, as she shook with sobs, her tears fell onto his bare arm and made him start. They were as cold as ice. And on her sleeve, where the apparition had brushed past her, there was dried blood.

Sara remained stubborn; nothing Mark could say would convince her to leave before she knew what was hidden behind the second door. The operation was then two weeks away.

Mark has been criticised for not acting sooner, and by no one more fiercely than himself, but he did everything he could to get her away. It was obvious to anyone that she was in no condition for surgery, even to herself much of the time, and he was prepared in the end to do anything to get her to leave – even to kidnap her if need be. But events overtook him.

We all know the ending to Sara's story, or we think we do. It has been told often enough, in newspapers and magazines, on TV and radio, in court, on stage, in bars and pubs and in our own homes. What happened is one thing; why it happened, how it happened is another. The usual view – certainly the view of the courts – is that Sara was either forced or fooled, perhaps both. There is another view, however – that she was complicit in her own fate – that she made a deliberate sacrifice for the sake of her own ambition. Unthinkable though it may seem, it is something that we do know she at least considered at one point during the following week, as is shown in this, the final entry in her video diary over this period.

Sara — 30 June 2005

(Sara is kneeling on her bed, looking into the camera, which is evidently balanced on a shelf. She seems to be looking into the screen, which she must have turned outwards so that she can watch her face as she speaks.)

I wouldn't mind, you know.

(She turns her face this way and that, examining it.)

What's in a name, what's in a face? It's just how you look. It'd be like me up there, then. All those people looking at me and adoring me and copying me and wanting to be me. It'd be like being two people. Well, not really, but that's not the point. It's not who you are, it's what people think you are. It's not what you do, it's what people do to you. Can you imagine the thoughts they'd have thinking about Sara Carter? Or what they'd feel?

(She smiles.)

I'd have done it, then. I'd be something else. My story would go right around the world. The girl who became Jonathon Heat. The girl who gave away her beauty. It's like a fairy story. They'd be telling it to children in their cradles a hundred years from now. Everyone would know who I am. Everyone! Except me, perhaps.

(She touches her scar.)

It'd be good if he kept that, though.

(Pause, while she looks at herself.)

What would it be like, do you think, to be able to put on a different one from time to time, or to try out another appearance like you take clothes on and off? It might be fun. Your face is yourself. If you change your face, do you change yourself, too? I think you do. I think you become someone else. Because, you know what? I wouldn't mind changing that, either.

(Pause.)

But I won't let him.

(She reaches out and turns the camera off.)

The Return of Bernadette

Overseas in Jamaica, as she released large sums of money to various charities and good causes with which she had little or no contact, Bernadette was feeling increasingly anxious about what was going on back at home. She was supposed to be caring for the girl afterwards – surely she should be there for the operation itself? Why was she being kept out of the way? Just to countersign a cheque once every few weeks?

It troubled her that Jonathon obviously regarded her as so easily put to one side when he wanted her gone. She had been away now for nearly two months and for a while had been successful in putting it out of her mind. But now, as the operation approached, it had begun to trouble her again. Bernadette is a person who does not like to make a fuss, but she is also a woman of conscience, and her conscience had started to bother her a great deal.

After I'd finished my interview with Bernadette in Bristol, the minister shook me by the hand and said this of her: 'She has the most extraordinary instincts; she always knows exactly what's going on. But she never believes it until after it's all happened.'

Bernadette flapped her hand at him and laughed the suggestion away, but I think he may have got it right. Either way, on the evening of 29 June, or thereabouts, she's not quite sure, she phoned Sara on her mobile, something she hadn't done for several weeks, and asked her a question.

'Have you seen any more of that ghost?' she wanted to know.

'Once or twice,' replied Sara. But Bernadette knew at once from something in her voice that the girl was frightened. There and then, she decided she was going home.

She didn't tell Jonathon that she was coming home early – he would certainly have ordered her not to. He had kept her away from the house whenever there was any surgery going on there, claiming that he couldn't bear the chilly atmosphere that existed whenever she had to work with Dr Kaye. Bernadette tended for years to believe whatever nonsense Heat cared to tell her, but even she had come to the conclusion that he kept her away so that he could go mad on his own without her interference. Maybe that was his business, maybe not, but now someone else was involved, a young girl who needed someone to keep an eye out for her in the absence of her parents. Bernadette couldn't see anyone except her who would do the job, so, reluctantly and very late in the day, she took it on for herself.

'I was too late of course,' she said. 'And that's no one else's fault but mine.' Nothing anyone there could say could convince her otherwise.

Bernadette didn't bother going home to Manchester, but went straight to her flat at Home Manor Farm.

Of course, once she was in the house, Heat was on to her in a moment. She was in the bath when the phone rang.

'Bernadette,' he said softly. 'To what do we owe this pleasure?'

She knew she was in trouble when he called her Bernadette. She was Bernie normally.

'I have a week before the next time they need me. I thought I'd come home and see how things were,' she told him.

'It's not a very convenient time,' said Heat.

Bernadette took a deep breath and came straight to the point. 'It's Sara, she's scaring me.'

There was a silence, into which Bernadette felt compelled to speak.

'This surgery, Jonathon. She's so *young*.'

Heat sighed irritably. 'She has that scar, it's only natural she wants it. Exactly because she's young and beautiful.'

'She's beautiful enough.'

'There's no such thing,' said Heat, 'as too much beauty.'

'. . . and you're letting that old butcher on her, I can't believe it,' burst out Bernadette. 'Mr Heat, if you have to do this, take her to a proper clinic,' she pleaded. What was the point of beating about the bush? She'd already shown her cards.

'We've been through this before,' said Heat coldly. 'It's none of your business. You should have stayed away.'

'I'm a trained nurse.'

166

'In this house,' pointed out Jonathon, 'you're a charity case.' At that point, she knew exactly how furious he was.

Lying in the bath, Bernadette listened to her employer's breath coming down the phone. He was waiting for her apology. All her instincts were to give it to him, and then to catch the next plane back to where she had come from. But although she so much loathed a fuss, her conscience in the end – at last! – was stronger.

'Mr Heat,' she said quietly, 'Dr Kaye has not got his full share of human kindness. And you, Jonathon, you're a sick man. Between you, you could do that girl a great deal of harm. You're a bad combination. Sara deserves better.'

She heard Heat catch his breath. It had been a long time since she had spoken to him like that.

'I'm sorry, Mr Heat,' she said, 'but that's the way I feel.'

At that point, Bernadette was expecting to be sacked and to be told to leave the house. But Heat seemed at a loss.

'I see. I see,' he stammered. After so many years of everyone doing as he told them, her words had taken his breath clean away.

'I'll have to report my concerns to Dr Kaye, of course,' she said quickly. 'And,' she added, 'to any other appropriate authority.'

There was a cold silence. Bernadette had really done it now. If there was one thing Heat could not abide, it was members of his personal staff taking information outside the house.

'I don't need to remind you that you signed a confident-iality clause in your contract before you came to work for me, Bernadette,' he said coldly.

'I'm not talking about the magazines, Mr Heat. I'm talking about professional bodies.'

'It makes no difference to me who it is,' said Heat. 'Just so long as you don't. I'll speak to you later,' he said, and put down the phone, unable to continue speaking to her.

Bernadette jumped out of the bath, pulled on some clean clothes without even bothering to dry herself, and ran up to see if Sara was ill.

She found Sara in her room, wearing her Heat mask and watching TV. On a table near the window was a little iced cake, which Jonathon had sent up with her breakfast. He was concerned that she wasn't eating enough – she was still losing weight despite the best efforts of her dietician, and he was forever tempting her with bits and pieces.

As soon as she saw who it was., Sara flew off the bed to hug her.

'Bernie! Oh, I wasn't expecting you back. Have you finished in Jamaica already? It's lovely to see you.'

Bernadette was touched. She'd forgotten how fond she'd become of Sara in such a short time. She hugged her back and lifted up the mask so she could kiss her. Sara accepted the kiss but pulled the mask quickly back down – a bad sign as far as Bernie was concerned, but she said nothing about it. They sat on the bed and caught up with their gossip. When questioned further about the apparitions, she skirted round the question without really saying anything. She had a little fridge in her room and she made Bernie tea and cut her a slice of cake. She had a little herself, tucking little finger-bites in under her mask.

'Take it off, let me see who I'm talking to,' Bernie chided her, but Sara shook her head.

'You haven't had another accident, have you?'

'No!' insisted Sara indignantly. Quickly, she lifted the mask so that Berme could see, before slipping it back down.

'A pretty girl like you,' said Bernadette.

'Flatterer,' Sara scolded. 'I just feel comfortable with it,' she added. She'd been making up the mask before Bernie came, a pretty face with soft colours. The makeup bag was still on the table. Now she began idly to make up the icing on the cake.

'You'll ruin it,' snapped Bernadette. Sara looked at her in surprise; Bernie bit her tongue. She was anxious. It was making her nag – an old fault.

She got up and stood behind Sara, watching her draw, an ugly face this time, on the iced surface of the cake. Then she bent down and whispered in her ear.

'You're not going to go through with this operation, you silly girl, are you? Tell me you're not. I'm going out of my mind worrying.'

Sara turned her face round to her again and murmured, 'Careful, Bernie – the cake might be bugged.'

'I'm being serious.'

'So am I. Sorry, Bernie,' she added quickly, seeing that she was upset. She gestured to the older woman to bend closer and whispered right into her ear.

'I won't even be here,' she said.

Bernie looked at her, trying to work out whether or not to believe her. She thought not, but, anyway, decided to take it at face value.

'Thank God!' she exclaimed in a loud voice, which made Sara frown. Bernadette bent down again and whispered, 'When are you going? Do you want me to come with you?'

Sara touched the side of her nose. 'Is berra you don't know,' she said, in a heavy, mock-Japanese accent. She glanced sideways at Bernie. 'What if I'm being kept prisoner here?'

'Oh, Sara, just stop it!' exclaimed Bernadette. It was all proving too much for her. She was jet-lagged after her flight – she'd come straight from the airport to the house and she'd had no chance to catch up on her sleep yet – and upset after her confrontation with Jonathon. Now Sara, whom she'd come all this way to see, was playing games with her. She couldn't help it: tears sprang up in her eyes.

Sara stared at her in surprise. She jumped up, pushed up her mask, embraced her and gave her a big kiss, right on the lips.

'Real lips for you, Bernie,' she whispered as she had once done before. 'Don't worry. It's sorted.'

The two of them stood face to face for a moment, then Sara took a step back, lifted the mask right off and turned her face to one side to show the mark the iron had left on her.

'Do you think I could be pretty again?' she asked.

'You're pretty now!'

'Oh yes – really, Bernie, that's not serious. But, actually, I don't mind about not being pretty. Maybe I should keep the scar. Do you think a boy would still want me like this? Or would he just pretend?'

'Only a silly boy would need to pretend.'

'Yes, but boys are silly, aren't they?'

'You won't get a silly boy, sweetheart,' said Bernadette, wiping away her tears. 'You'll get a lovely boy, a sensible boy. As for the scar, who cares? But if you do care,' she went on quickly, thinking that Sara really did, 'you can get it fixed. But not by Dr Ghoul.' She fixed Sara with an eye, put on her stern face and wagged a finger. 'Clear? Is it a deal? OK?' she said.

Sara laughed and slipped the mask back into position. 'Deal. Clear. OK,' she affirmed. She patted Bernie affectionately, like a dog. 'It's so good you're back,' she said. 'So, so good. I missed you. You're about the only person I can talk to round here.'

They embraced. Bernie felt a little better. Sara left her and walked over to her dressing table, where she wiped her mask clean of make-up and began to apply another face, while Bernie watched with distaste.

Sara loved decorating the masks; she spent hours at it. She had a big collection of permanent masks that she'd done in all sorts of designs, sometimes using glitter and delicate curling lines, sometimes jags and bruises and eye patches that turned the masks into pirates, victims of violence or characters from a manga mag. But she liked putting make-up on the plain ones, too.

'Let me have my fun,' said Sara.

'Some fun,' said Bernie. A thought occurred to her.

'You haven't told Jonathon you're not going through with it yet, have you?'

Sara paused; Bernie caught a look of alarm. But there was no way she could avoid the truth. 'Not yet,' she said. There was a slight shrug. She turned away and looked back in the mirror. 'I'm going to tell him tomorrow,' she said.

Bernie frowned. 'Well, that's not very fair to him, is it? After everything he's done.'

Sara turned to look at her. 'Why?' she asked. 'Why's it not fair?'

Bernadette paused. She wasn't actually sure why it wasn't fair. 'He's paying for it, he's setting it all up. Heavens, girl,' exclaimed Bernadette. 'The operation is in two weeks. Don't you think you ought to let them know?'

Sara pulled a face. Delighted though she was to see her, Bernadette was proving a problem. By chance, she and Mark had chosen to find out what was behind the second door that very night. Under her bed, her bag was already packed. It was all planned. They were going to go over the wire – she didn't believe for a moment that Heat would just let them go. And now Bernadette had come back, making this big fuss about the operation. She could blow the whole thing.

She turned back to her mirror with a shrug as if she didn't care. 'Tomorrow,' she said. 'I will tell him. Just – not quite yet.'

'But why not?'

'Does it matter? Honestly, Bernadette, don't make such a fuss. I'll tell him tomorrow, OK?'

Bernadette paused. She was certain she wasn't being told everything – but she didn't like to make a fuss. After all, why not? One more day. There was time. The operation wasn't due for another couple of weeks. So she let it ride, even though her instincts told her not to – a decision she has regretted ever since. Sara rolled her eyes, as if to say, Great! Big deal. She picked up a lip brush, leaned into the mirror and began applying a thin red line round the mask's lips. Somehow it went down into a jagged snarl at the side.

'It's a ghost story,' she said. 'I'll tell you all about it tomorrow. 'She added another jagged line. 'Now,' she said, 'I have to make myself pretty for my session with Dr Kaye the face-eater.'

Sometimes Sara made up her masks to look pretty, sometimes angry, sometimes downright strange if that's how she felt. On that morning of her last day, she made up a particularly bizarre face. She had one eyebrow right up in the air, the other drawn down low over her eye, and a manic, crooked smirk round the mouth that gave her an expression of manic disbelief – as if you'd just said something so ridiculous to her that it was about to drive her insane. She'd hardly finished when there was a knock at the door and one of the maids came in with her arms full of fresh bed linen. She jumped a mile when she saw, and dropped the bedding.

'Sara' she said, clutching her breast. 'You'll be the death of me. What are you like?'

'Nah hahahaha,' cackled Sara, like a demented demon. She turned to Bernie, filled with glee. 'And the old face-eater won't dare say a word,' she exclaimed. 'Let's get me dressed.' She bent down to pick up the linen, which she thrust into the arms of the maid and ran back to her dressing room with Bernadette close behind.

Getting dressed had been a big part of Sara's life when she first came to Home Manor Farm. Even before she moved in there were shopping trips with Heat in which he spent thousands of pounds on clothes for her.

As a result, Sara had a whole room full of clothes and shoes at Home Manor Farm and at first she got a huge amount of pleasure out of them, spending hours parading up and down in front of the full-length mirrors, getting Bernie or Heat or Janet, or anyone else who was around, to watch.

That morning, as every morning, Sara had an appointment with Dr Kaye to help her prepare for surgery and adapt to her new life, the life Heat was promising her was about to begin as soon as her face was sorted out – a life lived out in the blaze of celebrity. She told Bernie that morning that she wanted to take the chance to give the doctor one final grand wind-up. That bizarre face, with one surprised eyebrow up in the air and one scowling down by her eye, and that half ferocious, half hilarious smirk had set her off. She now spent a very enjoyable half hour choosing what to wear with it.

Normally, Bernadette would have made her dress properly for such an appointment; now she was just relieved that Sara wasn't taking it seriously. But she wasn't happy with the promise she'd been given. She knew how volatile Sara was. Why the delay? What if she changed her mind again?

Sara constantly tried clothes on while Bernadette alternatively laughed at her, scolded her, begged and bullied her to come clean about the operation in her meeting with Dr Kaye that very day. Sara was getting more and more annoyed with her fretting and by the time Dr Kaye came to collect her they were both thoroughly cross. As a result, Sara went down on her own, leaving Bernie up in her room, fuming and scared, and still none the wiser about what, exactly, Sara was planning to do. In the past she had attended Sara's session with the doctor and had been intending to attend this one, too. She said as much to the doctor when he knocked on Sara's door, but he'd put her off.

'I'd like to see Sara on her own this morning,' he told her. 'Mr Heat has informed me of your concerns and I've made another appointment for you at twelve thirty, if that's suitable.'

Bernadette pursed her lips and tipped her head back. 'Given the nature of my concerns, Doctor,' she said, 'I think I ought to attend now.'

The doctor's face gave nothing away. There was a pause, a stand-off, which was broken by Sara herself.

'I'd like to see Dr Kaye on my own today,' she said pertly. 'I have some private things to discuss with him.' She tipped her masked head at Bernadette, who stared impassively back; she was certain the girl was secretly putting her tongue out at her, or laughing at her, or worse. The doctor nodded.

'See you at twelve thirty, then,' he said to Bernadette.

There are photographs of Sara in the mask she made up that morning for her appointment with Dr Kaye. It's an amazing creation, which gives her a ferocious expression of amazement and disbelief so exaggerated that she looks like something out of a cartoon. She's wearing a scarlet dress, very short, which stuck out at the sides like a cone, with a loose vest bodice on top, and a pair of bright blue trainers with wedge soles. The dress was so short she was flashing the red bicycle shorts she wore underneath with every step she took.

What Dr Kaye thought of the whole arrangement is unknown. A secretive man, with no family, who had been deserted by his colleagues as his work with Jonathon Heat spiralled out of control, he kept himself to himself. For the last five years of his life, the only real conversations he had were with Jonathon Heat himself.

We do know that he kept extensive records and that there were notes towards a book he was planning to write, in which he was going to outline his practices and visions for cosmetic surgery in the future. He'd made claims to various people that once this book was published, the world of surgery would never be the same again. The notes for that book, along with all his notes about Heat, Sara and anyone else he may have secretly operated on since moving into Home Manor Farm, were destroyed in the fire that killed him. His only interviews are a couple with the police, in which he gave nothing away at all.

Like so much to do with Dr Kaye, what transpired between him and Sara on that day remains in the dark. We do know that when she came back to her room, a little over two hours later, Sara was badly upset. Bernadette was waiting for her, having avoided the best efforts of Heat and his staff to locate her, by turning off her mobile and hiding in the bathroom. She had everything she needed right there. People came in and out a couple of times, and she heard her name called a few times, but no one thought to look in there. She heard Sara come in but when she went out to greet her, Sara ran past her into the bathroom. But she didn't lock the door and Bernie followed her in.

'What is it? What's the matter? No, don't turn away. Now tell me, Sara, please. What's wrong?'

Sara was sitting in front of the mirror, pretending that everything was all right, but as soon as Bernie touched her, she stood up, burst into tears and flung her arms round her.

'Now, now. What've they done to you this time?'

Sara held tight and sobbed. It was sometime before she was able to speak.

There has been a great deal of debate about what exactly so upset Sara that day. The prosecution against Heat successfully argued that she was not well enough to give evidence in court and no one since has had the opportunity of asking her. As a result, different versions abound. One is what Jonathon Heat later told detectives – that Dr Kaye was simply satisfying himself yet again that Sara did indeed want to go through with the surgery, and was psychologically ready for it. Heat claimed he joined them once the session had ended, and that they had both pressed her perhaps more strongly than they should have done, because they knew Bernie was on the loose. Kaye was of the opinion that Bernadette could do a great deal of damage to Sara psychologically, with her strong religious views and her irrational opposition, as he saw it, to any sort of surgical intervention.

'I think we may have pressed her too hard in our eagerness to make sure she really wanted to go ahead,' said Heat. 'We wanted to cover ourselves against any future accusations, I suppose. Looking back, I can see that we were wrong to do that.'

Afterwards, the three of them had gone on a tour of medical facilities at Home Manor, including the operating theatre where the procedure was to take place. Sara kept her mask on throughout, but Heat claims that he saw how upset she was. Again he spoke to her about it, reassuring her that if she had any doubts at all, she only had to say and the operation would be put off or postponed.

'But she insisted she wanted to go ahead,' said Heat. 'Afterwards, I had a private word with Dr Kaye. We were both concerned about Sara's mental health, and I suggested postponing the operation. He assured me that putting it off would be far more damaging to her than going ahead.'

When the tour was over, in the operating theatre itself, Kaye produced the legal forms that Sara needed to sign to give him permission to operate. They had already been signed by Sara's mother, Jessica; now it was Sara's turn. According to Heat, she signed them without complaint and then went back to her room.

That's Heat's story. The story Sara told Bernadette is different.

'He was putting pressure on her to bring the operation forward and she was scared, because of what he'd done to Jonathon's face,' said Bernadette. 'They frightened her into going ahead as soon as possible. When she saw the operating theatre, I guess it all came home to her what she was doing and she panicked. That's what she told me.'

Which of these is true, or both, or something else, we shall never know unless Sara breaks her silence on the subject.

Sara leaned forward and shook with sobs on the older woman's shoulders. The mask was getting in the way, and she pulled it off and put it down on the washbasin so she could bury her head into Bernie's shoulder more easily. Bernie was touched.

'Oh, you lovely girl,' she exclaimed, and hugged her to her breast. Sara squeezed tighter and sobbed harder.

Bernadette decided there and then that enough was enough.

'That's it. Now you're coming with me,' she declared. She pushed Sara away and looked into her eyes as if to communicate her resolution to her, but Sara twisted away. She ran her arm across her streaming eyes, shook her head and ran off to sit at her dressing table, trying to clean herself up with tissues.

'Sara, what is this?' begged Bernie. She was much more upset than the story she was telling would seem to warrant. But Sara only shook her head, glancing at Bernadette in the mirror. She was getting in control of her tears now.

179

'But I can't go yet. Stop it, I told you not to worry. I have some things to do first.'

'What things?' demanded Bernie, but Sara shook her head. Bernadette cast her eyes to heaven, not certain how to proceed. She could hardly pick the girl up and carry her away against her will.

'Sara,' she said. 'I came all this way to help you. Why won't you tell me what's going on?'

'It's private. Why can't you all just leave me alone?' snapped Sara.

'I can't believe Dr Kaye would let you go ahead if he could see how upset you are just now.'

Sara rubbed her face and moaned to herself. Bernadette waited patiently for a response.

'OK,' she said. 'OK. If I tell you, will you give me one more day? Promise!'

Bernadette stood for a moment, then she shook her head. 'I can't make that promise, Sara, I can't,' she said. 'I have to do what I think is best for you. You're asking me to say that I might not do that, and I can't say it.'

Sara stamped her foot in frustration. Bernadette seemed so mild and kind and willing to please, but her principles had been quietly bolted to the floor. She was immovable.

But Sara must have thought that Bernadette was going to go to Dr Kaye and tell him everything she'd said about quitting the operation. Believing as she did that he was trying to steal her face, that was very dangerous indeed. Perhaps that's why she told her what she did.

'You remember that morning the day you left?' she said at last.

'The ghost you saw!' exclaimed Bernadette, and her heart began banging like a drum. Ever since she was a little girl and her grandmother told her terrifying stories back in Jamaica, she had been scared of ghosts.

'Well – I found her,' said Sara. She beckoned Bernadette over to the bed, opened a drawer and took out a photograph, which Bernadette later identified as the one Sara had filmed in her video diary. At the time, she recognised it as one that used to hang on the wall in a downstairs corridor. Sara tapped the glass with her nail. 'It's her. Look. Do you know her?'

Bernie peered over the photograph and gasped. The face looking out at her was the spitting image of Sara.

'Oh my God, Sara, it's you,' she whispered.

'Now then,' said Sara. 'What do you suppose that means?'

Bernie was in a state of terror, although she couldn't exactly say why. She looked closer. 'But it can't be,' she said.

'Can't it?' said Sara. 'Perhaps not, especially since it was taken before I ever came here.'

Bending over the glass, Bernie examined the other faces. She recognised them, as well. In fact, this was an old staff photograph, taken on one of the days out that Heat organised for his people from time to time.

And then she knew who the girl was.

'No, it's not you at all,' she said. 'That's Katie. She used to work here.'

'What happened to her?' asked Sara in an even voice.

181

Bernie shrugged. 'She left.'

'Suddenly?'

'A lot of people work here, Sara. I can't remember what happened to them all.'

'It's important,' insisted Sara. Bernie thought about it, but shook her head.

'Do you remember her surname?' asked Sara, but Bernie couldn't remember that, either.

'Well, it was her. And, if it was her, that means . . . well, you know what that means, don't you?'

'Stop it!'

'It means she's dead.'

'You talk nonsense.'

Together they stood and stared at the small face smiling out at them. The girl really did look extraordinarily like Sara.

Sara turned away. 'Now you know,' she said. She went into the bathroom to wash her face.

Bernadette was so terrified after this conversation, she hardly knew what was going on. She felt as if the ghost was on her heels, after her blood, about to jump in through her mouth the second she opened it. But she also felt very strongly that Sara was manipulating her in some way. She'd had enough.

Without a word, she turned and ran down the corridors to her own room, where she sat on the bed and cried. In a little while, Sara came and banged on the door, begging to be let in, but Bernie stayed where she was until the noise stopped. She went to the bathroom for a wash and to fix her face. After waiting a little longer to be sure she was on her own, Bernadette opened the door and left to keep her appointment with Dr Kaye.

As Bernadette tiptoed past Sara's room on her way to Dr Kaye, Mark was tucked away in his little room in a building nearly a mile away from the house, testing a small device he'd made for that night's adventure.

Mark, too, was determined that Sara was getting out of that house as soon as possible. Her visions and plans had him all in a whirl; he didn't know what to believe and what to disbelieve, but he knew that she had to get out of that place and if he had to shoot his way out, if he had to hit her over the head and kidnap her, she was going. He was going to rescue her whether she wanted him to or not.

The device he was trying out was an attachment to a digital video camera that fitted onto the lens and was narrow and flexible enough to push through the crack under the door. There was a little bulb just strong enough to cast a bleary glow of light, and optical fibres that would carry the images back to the lens. The camera itself had an infrared setting. He and Sara would be able to crouch outside the door, see what was inside, record it, and take it away as evidence.

Sara, of course, never made it away that night, but, as far as we can tell, she was ready to do it at that point. Her bag was packed, waiting under her bed for her. Mark had a friend coming to pick them up from an agreed place outside the gates at an agreed hour. It was all set.

And there was another person involved, and another part

of the plan that Mark knew nothing about. Janet, sitting miles away in Manchester, was the second accomplice.

For some weeks now, Sara had been in touch with various magazines and newspapers – *OK* magazine, the *Daily Mirror, Heat,* the *Sun,* the *Daily Mail,* the *News of the World, Now!* – all those. She'd proved to them that she was for real by giving them inside details about Heat and his house and entourage not available to the general public, and warned them that something big was about to happen – but not what, and not when, either. Just that it was imminent, that it was very big and that it would destroy Heat. Janet's role was to alert them. Sara had even posted her a separate mobile phone to make calls on, to allay Janet's fears of being traced. When Sara came out of Home Manor Farm, she wanted the world's media to be there to watch it happen. She wanted to come on live TV.

'It was to be her big launch,' remembered Janet. But she didn't know everything. Sara hadn't abandoned her plans for fame at all – just changed them. Not with Jonathon Heat, but by exposing him. The world's press was going to be there to see her do it.

Meeting with Dr Kaye

As a surgeon, we know a great deal about Wayland Kaye, but as a man, he is almost as difficult to know as Sara herself. There is of course the image of him we get from the newspapers – the ruthless doctor, prepared to commit any crime to try out his theories and save his reputation. Heat has encouraged this view, claiming ignorance and blaming Kaye for the whole thing. Although the courts decided otherwise, it's a view that remains widespread.

Never a popular man, or a sociable one, Kaye seems to have taken his falling out of fashion and repute with the medical profession back in the seventies deeply to heart. He never really managed to turn his colleagues into friends – he was too obsessive to be good company – but now he withdrew totally, cutting himself off and refusing to discuss his theories with anyone in case they used them and stole the credit. There had been a marriage in his early twenties that lasted a few years, but Kaye seems to have been more interested in men sexually. There was no partner and, as far as we can tell, not even any close friends who were gay.

He even told one colleague at work that he despised gay culture. He went cruising around the gay haunts in Manchester a couple of times a month, but rarely went with the same man twice and, as far as we know, never took any of his lovers home.

Our knowledge of his life over the next two decades is vague. We do know that the police have recently reopened a murder investigation from the late nineties, and that Kaye's name has been associated with this, so far without any real evidence. Readers may remember the cases, known in the press as 'the faceless corpses', due to the murderer's habit of taking the skin of the corpse's face before abandoning the body. The implication is obvious: Kaye may have been continuing his experiments on unwilling victims.

When he met Jonathon Heat and found the rock star receptive to his vision, it must have seemed like a godsend to Kaye. He was over seventy by this time, and had abandoned any hope of ever continuing his work or escaping from the reputation of failure and eccentricity he'd picked up twenty years before. Now, at last given the chance to carry out his ideas, the results were spectacular. Kaye seemed to be able to do anything he wanted, a veritable magician in flesh. There were, of course, voices of dissent, professional voices, who claimed that what he was doing was not backed up by proper research and that things could go wrong at any moment... but in the light of the kind of results he was producing, the public put it down to professional jealousy.

Kaye was back on the lecture circuit and enjoying every minute of it. Film stars, musicians and politicians courted him. He had signed an exclusivity contract with Heat for five years, but there was by all accounts a huge list of people who wanted him to work on them once he was free of it. Personal relationships still eluded him, however. He was not popular with the other members of staff at Home Manor Farm, and continued to hold himself aloof from other members of his profession. It seems that over all the years his only close relationship was with Heat himself and, according to all witnesses, the only thing they ever talked about was surgery.

When, in the course of a few weeks in April 2003, Heat's face collapsed, Kaye was once again confronted with failure. This time, the failure walked and talked and paid him his money. Kaye became more withdrawn than ever. Sara, of course, had daily therapy sessions with him and it may be that she could say more about him, if she was willing or able. The records that Kaye apparently kept went with him to the grave in the fire that destroyed all evidence of his professional and personal past.

Kaye, at the time of his interview with Bernadette, in the last week of his life, was a tallish man, somewhat stooped with age. He was eighty-two. He dressed at all times of the day in his white coat, as if the house itself was his hospital and his day's work never ceased. He had a high forehead which was very deeply lined, both sideways and across, which gave him an alarming appearance – as if, in the words of one member of staff, 'he had been scoured with a knife'.

Bernadette and Dr Kaye had never had an easy relationship, but it had once been much better than it now was. She was deeply suspicious of what he had been able to do with Jonathon when things were going well, and since the collapse of her employer's face, in common with the rest of the staff, she had come to loathe him with a vengeance. He had once boasted to her that 'success can justify most things', a statement that Bernadette actively despised.

And yet despite all this, and against all reason, you may think, she must have maintained some respect for him at least. Bernadette's aim in that meeting was to convince the doctor that Sara was mentally unfit to give her consent to go ahead with the operation. Kaye always put great emphasis on professionalism and Bernadette believed that if she could cast doubt upon the patient's mental state, he would cancel or at least postpone things. Why she should have thought this is difficult to see; she had tried before and failed to do the same thing with Heat, and is on record as saying that she never once knew Dr Kaye consider anyone unsuitable for surgery. But Bernadette is an optimist. She believed in her own arguments and hoped that, as one professional to another, he would listen to her, regardless of their personal relationship.

Dr Kaye sat quietly behind his desk, his tape recorder running, occasionally taking notes as she talked. She did her best to reach him that day, but Kaye remained as he always was, always had been – distant, professional, unreadable. Having told him her own doubts, she went on to talk about Sara's. She told him everything she knew. She reminded him of the report she had made before she left for Jamaica, about Sara seeing ghosts with no face, wearing her clothes. She told him that Sara now believed that it was the ghost of a girl who had once worked here – 'Katie someone,' she said – and that she believed this girl had died or perhaps even been killed here in the house.

And she told him that Sara had told her she was not planning on going ahead with the operation.

'She told me she desperately wants it,' replied Dr Kaye.

Bernadette stared at him across the desk. She licked her lips. 'But, surely, just the fact that she's telling us different things, Doctor…' she began.

Kaye raised his eyebrows doubtfully. 'I'm her counsellor, Mrs McNalty,' he pointed out. To which Bernadette, who out of the two of them had had far more training as a counsellor than he had, could find no reply.

At one point, Bernadette leaned across the table and appealed to him as a person.

'What's wrong with you these days, Doctor? I never see you smile any more,' she said – which, as she pointed out herself, was a bit rich, since Dr Kaye rarely smiled anyway.

But he did now carefully and rather ruefully, she thought.

'Too many cares, Bernadette,' he said quietly. 'I should have retired years ago.'

'Then why don't you?'

'I can't leave him like that.'

'I'm not talking about him, Doctor. I'm talking about this young girl. She's just seventeen! She might need a new bit of skin on her face, but no more than that. New boobs and a new tummy and a new nose – what's that all about? At seventeen? It's crazy.'

'Times have changed, Bernadette,' he told her. 'Young girls dream of operations like this. It's like buying new clothes these days.' Again, he gave her that rueful smile. 'I never met a woman yet who liked her body. Now, for the first time, it's possible to have anything you want.'

'That's all back to front,' declared Bernie. 'If they put real women in the magazines and on the TV, instead of made-up people, those girls would know how lovely they already are, without getting cut up and turned into tailors' dummies.'

'Politics isn't my business,' said Kaye, and he spread his hands as if to say, This world! It just keeps on turning...

'Wayland,' said Bernadette. He raised his eyes to look directly at her. She'd never used his name before. 'She's a sick girl. Let her go!'

'I don't hold her, Bernadette. It's her own choice. All she has to do is tell me not to and I won't. It's that simple.'

'But she's a sick girl!'

'Not in my opinion.' He paused. 'Not in the way you think, anyway.'

The interview continued. Bernadette was appalled at the lack of progress she was making.

'I have to tell you, Doctor, that I think all of this is very unprofessional.'

'It will all be looked into thoroughly,' he told her.

'By who? By you? Since when is it professional practice to let the surgeon who is operating on her be her counsellor as well?'

'As the surgeon who is performing the operation, it's my business to decide if she's fit or not,' replied Kaye coldly.

Bernadette could hold her tongue no longer. 'Look what you did to Jonathon,' she spat. 'And now it's her turn, is it?'

Kaye closed his notebook. 'And now I think this interview is at an end.'

Bernadette blushed. She had been unprofessional herself, and apologised for her outburst. Kaye nodded. Then he leaned forward and picked up the phone. He spoke briefly into it.

'Jonathon would like you to wait here. He wants a word in person before things go any further,' he said.

Bernadette agreed. But first, she needed to use the toilet. She got up to leave the office, closed the door, and then, glancing quickly about to check that she wasn't being watched, leaned back with her ear to the door, to see if she could work out what Kaye was up to.

There was a slight movement and she heard the doctor speak.

'Happy?' he asked.

Bernadette jumped back, thinking he knew she was there, but there was no further noise. To whom the doctor was speaking, on his own, in an office that led to nowhere, is anyone's guess. Those who have argued that Heat was the driving force behind the terrible crime that was about to be committed have offered this as evidence that the doctor was being blackmailed. Perhaps he was speaking to the CCTV. There is every chance, in fact, that Heat had been watching the whole time.

***

Bernie was left waiting for almost an hour in Kaye's office. She was expecting Heat to come, but in the event it was Dr Houseland who turned up, one of Kaye's assistants, asking her to go through the whole thing again. Bernadette obliged, pleased to have the chance to put her views on record with someone other than Kaye himself, but a bit put out that she was having to go through the same thing all over again.

Dr Houseland – who, despite his name, claimed to be from Chile – like most of the medical staff at Home Manor Farm at that time, has never been traced. Bernadette had never seen him before, but that was nothing new; medical staff were always coming and going. In the fire that destroyed the house a few days later, there were the remains of three other bodies in the wreckage, each of which have denied all the efforts of modern science to identify them. Dr Houseland may have been one of those, or he may have been an occupant of one of the cars and light aircraft that left the estate later that night.

Houseland informed Bernadette that there were meetings going on at every level to try to sort out the process her complaints had put in motion. Heat himself, apparently, was going through a crisis of his own about the operation and it was highly likely that he would call it off whatever Dr Kaye thought. To Bernadette, that rang true. The idea that Heat himself was having doubts helped her believe that she was going to get her way.

Houseland also told her that Heat would be seeing her shortly, and Bernadette, revived by this information, was determined to convince him that cancellation was the right thing to do.

After the interview with Dr Houseland, Bernadette was again left on her own in the same office for another hour or so. A cup of tea, a sandwich and a slice of cake were brought to her. Then she was taken to another, smaller room where, after yet another long wait, she had an interview with Heat himself.

Bernadette felt very uncomfortable about this one. She had spent the last ten years of her life ministering to Heat, and in return he had shown her great generosity. Heat commanded enormous loyalty among his staff but it was an unspoken truth that to go against him was a blow to his person. Heat would not be angry; he would be devastated. The effect was that Bernadette felt like she was stabbing him in the back.

She knew at once that he'd been crying. His face, as usual, was hidden by the mask, but the glitter of his eyes gave it away.

'Jonathon,' she said. 'What have you got to cry about? It's not your face he's mucking about with this time.'

Heat blinked back his tears. He rarely sobbed, but the tears leaked down behind his mask throughout.

'I only want to help her, Bernie,' he said. 'You know that. Why is she so scared of me? Is it true? She never shows it to my face. I only wanted to help,' he repeated. He touched his face underneath the mask as he spoke. 'Is it this?' he asked.

He had been one of the most beautiful and talented men of his generation. Now everything he had was falling to pieces. What price fame now? thought Bernie, but she could never say such a thing to him.

Instead she came round the table to hug him. She never doubted his words then – she never doubts them to this day. He put his face into her bosom and wept.

'Jonathon,' she said. 'She loves you the same as all the rest of us. But she's scared. She isn't ready to go through with this. She's a sick girl – just like you've been sick, to have all this work done on yourself. Look at you! Do you want her to end up like you?'

Heat said nothing, but his body shook with silent tears.

'She needs better care than Dr Kaye can give her – and so do you. Why do I repeat myself? I've been saying this for years, but you never listen. If you want to help her, you can do it the same way as you can help yourself. You want a good psychiatrist. Look what you've done to yourself! You need help! You have to be careful – you're in danger of luring her down the road you took with Dr Kaye, with all your good intentions.'

'There's Dr Houseland,' said Heat. 'He thinks she's OK.'

'You need independent people,' said Bernadette firmly.

Bernadette talked; Heat nodded. From what she could gather, he was terrified of the same thing happening to Sara as had happened to him, but he was also terrified of that scar on her face that the iron had left there. It made him feel physically sick, he said.

'She's perfect, she's perfect,' he kept saying. 'But that scar's so ugly. She can't live with that.'

'But, if she's perfect, why do you want to change her?' said Bernadette.

'So she can be more perfect,' replied Heat.

They talked for over an hour. Heat was distraught, but willing to listen and he made several promises to Bernadette. One, that he would do his best to talk Sara out of all her operations except for the burn scar on her cheek; two, that he would postpone the operation in any event for a week or two at least; and three, that he would take her to see someone independent before any further decisions were made.

'A second opinion,' said Bernadette. 'Everyone should have a second opinion. Then you can decide.'

Bernadette was happy. Heat was a man of his word. In all her years working at Home Manor Farm, she'd never known him tell a lie.

'We've all got our pasts,' she told him, 'and we all have to live with them. All you ever know is, the future gets shorter and the past gets longer. I've got to get old, you've got to get old, she's got to get old. Do it gracefully, Jonathon – and let her do it gracefully as well.'

She was late – but she had started a process. Bernadette was convinced that she had won the day. But Heat had a price.

'I've made my promises to you, Bernie,' he said as he stood up to leave. 'Now I want one from you.'

'What is it?'

'I want you to promise me not to go public with any of this.'

'I can promise that, Jonathon. I've never dreamed of doing such a thing.'

'Good. Because if you do, I will pursue you, and your brothers and sisters, and your cousins and all their children and their children's children through the courts of any land they live in, and I'll strip them of any possessions they may own and any children they have the care of.'

The biblical terms of the threat took Bernadette's breath away, and she could only stare while Heat pulled his pashmina round his neck and stepped to the door.

'Dr Kaye would like another meeting, if you don't mind, Bernie,' he said mildly. 'If you'd just wait here.'

Then he was gone.

Several hours had passed already since making her original complaint. Bernadette was feeling frustrated at being isolated from events, especially from Sara, whom she felt she ought to talk to if only to let her know what she was doing and why. But she believed what she had been told, that Sara was being interviewed and reassessed in the light of what she had told Kaye. Nothing had happened that was untoward – in fact, the slow unfolding of events could be taken as a good sign, a sign of thoroughness. And so she sat on her own in the little interview room, waiting for the reappearance of Dr Kaye.

The room she was in was small, maybe four by three metres, but it was quite high – high enough for the only window in it to be out of reach. Up in the corner of the room, to her irritation, a CCTV camera stared relentlessly down at her. It seemed to follow her around like the eyes in a painting. All she could do was sit at the desk that nearly filled the little room, and fidget uncomfortably in its steady gaze.

Another cup of tea was brought to her by a maid, along with a pile of magazines to occupy her while she waited and an offer of food which she accepted. A little later, she was brought a plate of sandwiches. Again, she waited. Before long, she needed to leave the room to use the toilet again, but when she opened the door she found a very large gentleman outside, who accompanied her there and back, explaining that Mr Heat and Dr Kaye wanted to see her and let her know what action was being taken before she left. Shortly afterwards, when she explained to the large gentleman that she wanted to go for a walk, she was politely asked to stay where she was and to keep the door shut. Dr Kaye, or Heat, she was promised, would not be long. In the meantime there had been complaints about her and she was not at liberty to roam the house as she had before.

As he closed the door behind her, Bernie heard the quiet but unmistakable sound of a key turning in the door. She was locked in.

Gradually all Sara's jokes about Dr Ghoul the face-eater came back. Her own fear of Kaye, the strange, inconsistent ways of Jonathon Heat himself, the hours and hours of waiting without anything happening, took their toll. She now noticed that the window high in the wall not only didn't open but was made of thick bottle glass. The only other place she had seen such a window was in a cell at the police station. The door was a fire door, as solid as a tree trunk. Outside the door, in her own words, 'was a ten-foot gorilla.' Bernadette was, in effect, a prisoner.

As soon as she came to this conclusion, Bernadette was on her feet. If she was going to be kept prisoner – and God only knew what that meant – she wasn't going to sit there and take it. Enough time had been wasted. She leapt up and began pounding on the door with her fist, shouting to be let out. The key turned, the door was opened and she ran out and into the corridor, only to bang into the big man waiting outside for her.

'Mrs McNalty…' he began.

'What are you doing? Stand away – let me past!' she yelled.

The man looked wounded. 'Mrs McNalty!' he said. 'Dr Kaye will see you presently…'

'I have to go,' she insisted, and tried to push her way through. But the man was standing in the way, and now he began to walk slowly towards her, gently ushering her back into the room with his broad chest.

'Please, Mrs McNalty, I know you've been waiting a long time,' he explained reasonably, pushing away.

Bernadette kicked him very hard in the shin and then did something she had not done for nearly thirty years, when a young man proved too insistent outside a club in Brixton. She punched him in the balls.

The man bent over with a gasp of pain.

'Oooooh! Mrs McNalty!' he groaned. But Bernadette was already on her way up the corridor. The man, bent over double, hobbled after her, calling plaintively. He sank to his knees and began fumbling in his pocket for his mobile phone.

Bernadette is a large woman, not used to running, and by the time she reached the stairway going down she was gasping for air and had to pause, leaning against the banisters to catch her breath. Downstairs in the entrance hall groups of people were going to and fro, some of them loading various pieces of equipment into the elevators going down. Bernie stared in fascination as a couple of porters went past, one wheeling a trolley laden with oxygen bottles and the other with crates of surgical supplies.

Across the floor, she saw Heat at the centre of a small group, shaking hands with someone. He'd spotted her already, and was eyeing her above the heads crowding around. In a panic, Bernadette leapt down the stairs as fast as she was able and made a bolt for the door, but by the time she got there he was already waiting for her.

'Well, Bernie,' he said to her in his mellifluous voice. 'You've certainly stirred things up here, haven't you? Not like you at all.'

'Mr Heat.' Bernie clutched her throat and tried to hang on to her dignity, which breathlessness and fear were stealing from her. 'You had me locked in that room,' she accused.

'Dr Kaye... we both, really... felt it would be better. He's in charge. Of course, you're free to go if you want. Sara's in a terrible state. I know, I know...' He lifted his hands. 'But the fact is, Bernie, she was so calm before you came, so happy, and now she's in a dreadful state.' He shook his head. 'The operation will have to be postponed at the very least because of that alone, so you don't need to worry about that.'

'I think what you're doing is an evil thing, Mr Heat, for all your fame and money, and for all your kindness, too,' she said.

'I understand, Bernie, but it's very late in the day to decide that I'm a monster for something you agreed to yourself not so long ago.'

Bernadette stared at him. She couldn't even be bothered pointing out that she had never been happy with Sara's operation. She had shown her hand. She found herself looking suspiciously over his shoulder at the medical equipment being loaded up.

'Who are these people?' she asked.

Heat shrugged. 'Deliveries. This sort of stuff doesn't get here on the day, Bernie, you know that.'

'So are you telling me, Mr Heat, that the operation is called off?' she demanded.

'Yes.' Heat shrugged. 'Last I heard, anyway. They're talking to her now.'

'I want to see her.'

'I'm sorry, that's not possible. I haven't been allowed to see her, either.'

'I'm her nurse.'

Jonathon shook his head. 'But you're not,' he replied, and that was the truth.

Bernadette turned to go. Jonathon followed her to the door. On the steps she turned. 'You'll tell me as soon as you know?' she begged.

'We'll be in touch,' said Heat.

'When?'

'I can't say when. But we'll be in touch before anything goes ahead. The operation isn't for another couple of weeks anyway.'

'Will you ring me tonight? Let me know how things are going?'

Heat sighed impatiently. 'OK. I'll ring you tonight,' he agreed. He shook his head, obviously deeply saddened by Bernadette's sudden lack of trust.

It wasn't OK, but it was the best she was going to get. Heat nodded goodbye, Bernadette nodded back and made her way down the steps. When she got to the bottom, she looked back up to the ageing rock star. He was looking down to her, his chin forward, his scrawny, masked head looking more reptilian than ever as he peered down. She knew him well enough to tell that his lips – what was left of them – were drawn out in a grin that she supposed he hoped was a comforting smile, but the effect was that he looked more like a snake about to strike. What horrible secrets were going on behind those sunglasses? she wondered. What lives had those long pale fingers ruined?

Bernadette had never had such thoughts about her employer before, and now they took her completely by surprise. She had no idea where they came from. She staggered down the last few steps to the tarmac and walked unsteadily round to the car park behind the house, where she kept her vehicle. She had been more forward than she had ever been in her life, and now she felt utterly shattered. All she wanted was a hot bath, a bite to eat and her bed.

That afternoon, Sara spent several hours completely on her own – an unusual event during her time at Heat's house, perhaps the only time she had been alone for such a long period during her entire stay. As far as we know, no one disturbed her from one o'clock until almost four, when Jonathon Heat came in to discuss Bernadette's story with her. How she spent that time and what was going through her mind, we have no way of knowing.

Heat, according to his own testimony, told her that Houseland and Kaye were going to interview her to reassess if the operation should go forward or not. He stayed with her for over an hour, then left her while Kaye came in to interview her. Kaye himself was furious at this development so late in the day. Bernadette, in his opinion, had turned the whole carefully planned operation into a farce.

'She's a liability,' he told Heat, when they met to discuss what was happening earlier in the day. 'She's only here because you're overly sentimental. She's in the way.'

Kaye spent nearly two hours with Sara that day, some of the time with Dr Houseland, some of the time on his own, making tests and interviewing her. When he came out, he met up with Heat again to deliver his opinion.

'Sara was desperate for the operation to go ahead,' Heat reported some months later in court.

His testimony that day was confused – not surprising considering the condition he was in. In general, we have very little information as to what exactly Kaye's thoughts were, as regards Sara. Our main source of information is a brief report he prepared on the case early on, while Sara was still in hospital. The report is incomplete, but it does give some idea of how his mind was working at the time. His theories, as ever, were unusual to say the least.

Kaye appears to have seen Sara as a girl trapped behind her own face. Her dissatisfaction with her appearance was so profound, he believed, that she suffered from a permanent sense of self-alienation from her own body. Her anorexia was one aspect of this, her self-harming another. He describes her sense of identity as being so troubled that she only ever behaved as herself by impersonating herself. To Sara, her voice, her manner, even her appearance, were not her own.

He seems to believe that the operation he was planning, in which she would be involved in choosing her own looks, her own body, was her only chance of having a normal life.

Those were Dr Kaye's thoughts on the eve of Sara coming to stay at Home Manor Farm. There's no reason to think that they had changed in the interval. We do know that after extensive tests he arrived at the clear conclusion that cancelling or postponing the operation was the worst thing he could do to her. According to Heat, Kaye told him that the fuss Bernadette was making was having a detrimental effect on her, and he was concerned that it might push her into another episode of self-harm – possibly a very serious one. In the light of this, he decided to bring the operation forward to that very night. At the same time, he insisted that Bernadette be expelled from the house.

Heat agreed to both demands.

The Last Day

The strain of the past few weeks had left Mark in a state of feverish anxiety. Sometimes he was struck with a terrible certainly that Sara was right, that this was the house of a monster – that they should be running away, not creeping around the ogre's den in the middle of the night. To discover his dark secrets is a sentence of death.

Such thoughts terrified him, not so much for fear of his and Sara's lives, but because the rest of the time he found the whole nightmarish vision so incredible and unbelievable. How had things gone so far? Why had he allowed himself to be drawn into a world of madness against his own good sense? They were within a couple of weeks of the operation, Sara was obviously unwilling or unfit to go ahead with it – but here they still were, with foolish deeds to accomplish before she would set herself free.

Whenever he tried to talk to her about it, he came away with promises in his hand, but never for today. Now, at last, today had come.

It was all set. Mark had hung on to Woods's key long

enough to get a copy made, so the first door presented no problem. They had arranged to meet in her room at half past midnight and go down through the house together and make their final attempt to open the second door, or at least to see behind it. That done, they would flee.

Then, at eight o'clock, Sara rang. Things had changed; their plans had to be brought forward. She wanted him to pick her up at ten.

That was appalling. At half past midnight, the house would be more or less asleep; at ten, anyone could be around in the corridors – Woods or one of his men on security patrol, or Heat himself, who often wandered the house late at night when he couldn't sleep.

He texted her... 'Can't be done.'

She texted back. 'Must be!!!!!'

'Why?'

'!!!!!'

'It's too busy.'

'We have to. Mark, please.'

So he felt he had no choice.

It was a very different matter sneaking through a house that was still wide awake than through a sleeping one. Then, you just had to be quiet; now, you never knew what was round the next corner. Mark felt like a child sneaking out on a night-time naughtiness, afraid of being caught and sent to bed. But this was something else. What would happen if they were caught? Sacked? Told off? Murdered? Surely not the last. But his heart beat as if it knew something he didn't.

He found his way in through a window and picked his way slowly up to Sara's room, freezing the cameras one at a time, hiding behind each corner, listening. Twice he had to duck into a doorway when people came along, and on the second floor, where Sara slept, he was nearly caught by Tom Woods and a couple of his men, doing the rounds. They appeared suddenly at the end of a corridor he had just entered. Mark had to dash into a room with no time to check it, and found himself staring into the lens of camera watching behind the door. He turned his back to it, found it and froze it, but it was too late. He had been seen. If anyone was watching it right now, the alert would be out – the observer would be phoning Woods that very second, and he could expect the door to open any moment now.

He waited, not daring to breathe. Woods and his men approached – and passed. Someone in the control room had not been paying attention. But they would check as soon as they found Sara gone, and they would know. Heat would prosecute, without doubt.

But that was a trouble for another day. After a suitable pause, Mark crept out and carried on his way, stopping and starting like a mouse in a fox's den, until he arrived outside Sara's door. He knocked two quick, two slow, their secret signal, and went in.

He found Sara sitting at her dressing table, looking at herself in the mirror. He was surprised that she didn't leap up. She seemed rather subdued to him. She turned round to smile when he came in.

She got up. There was a bag by her feet. 'Now we go – we better hurry,' she said, dashing his faint hopes that she would change her mind.

'What's the problem?' he asked. 'Why can't we stick to the original plan?'

'Can't explain, we just have to go. I just want to be out of here by midnight. OK?'

He paused and then nodded. Anything was OK so long as she got out.

'Is that yours?' He glanced down at the bag in her hand in surprise. It was so small. Heat had bought her so much stuff – some weeks he had taken her out shopping almost every day. She used to say it was like things suddenly became free. It made them both laugh, the amount of stuff she owned these days, but she loved some of it and she'd been worrying about what to take and what not to. But now here she was with this little bag that just about held a toothbrush and few bits and pieces.

Sara shrugged. 'Things happen.' She paused. 'Things happen, and it makes you realise.' She gestured around the room with its opulence. 'It's all just . . . sweeties. Sweeties and shit. And you know what? This is shit, too.' She pulled at the skin on her face. 'It's what's in here that counts.' Sara held her hand over her heart, the spirit inside her, as if she was a treasure chest and real jewels shone within.

Mark gave her a crooked smile. 'This is all shit,' he said, waving his hand around the room. 'But you – you're never shit.'

They stood and looked into each other's eyes for a moment. Then Sara looked away.

'Let's go,' she said. She made for the door, then turned again.

'Have you got it?' she asked.

Mark lifted up the camera with the little attachment he'd made. Sara smiled, reached up to kiss his lips and walked to the door. She waited while Mark checked with his Palm Pilot. He nodded. She opened the door and they stepped outside.

They made it down to the service area, then along the sloping corridor that led to the locked door. As they walked, Mark noticed how Sara kept looking over her shoulder and checking her watch. Several times he asked her what was wrong, but she shook her head impatiently. He assumed it was the ghost and didn't think to ask if there was anything he needed to know.

They turned the corner into the final corridor. Again, she turned her head to look behind her.

'Is someone coming?' he asked, but she shook her head and headed off down the slope towards the locked door at a trot. Mark followed on.

As they got close Sara started doing it again – reacting to things he couldn't see. She made little jumps and starts, gasped, turned her head suddenly as if to look at something or moved to one side to let someone past who wasn't there. Mark found this whole performance unnerving, but he couldn't take his eyes off her. He felt like a blind man walking among wild beasts that only she could see.

Mark opened the first door with the copied key, then he got down at once on his knees, taking out his little video camera, trying to put the attachment on quickly and fumbling instead. Sara stood behind him, looking back down the corridor, jumping and twitching as unseen images and sounds assailed her. At last, he fitted the attachment, turned on the camera and slid it under the door. Despite Sara's certainty that there was something dark and dangerous behind the door, despite his own pounding heart, he was sure that he was going to see another empty room, just floor and walls hiding nothing, holding nothing in, holding no one prisoner. But, still, his heart told another tale. With Sara, you never knew. And, if she was right, then Heat, with all his nice manners and gentle ways, wasn't just someone to be despised. If she was right, he was a serial murderer.

If looks could kill. And perhaps his did.

There was a moment while the camera adjusted, then the display screen brightened. Sara bent down and rested her chin on Mark's shoulder to get a better look.

The flexible lens had gone under the door, but at an angle; it illuminated a view along the skirting boards, but, even so, they could see at once that this room was far bigger than any of the others they had looked in. Mark fiddled about with the lens. It twisted, flicking up and down on the floor and casting quick glances at the rest of the room. He caught a glimpse of machinery, digital displays and lit-up dials. Metal, an object of some sort, something on wheels. Machinery. Then the view stabilised.

There was a drip standing next to a bed in a corner – that was what was on wheels. The machines were medical monitors. Sara let out a little groan.

'So, it's true,' she whispered. Mark twisted round to look up at her. True? Did this prove her theories? In a flash he suddenly believed that it was true, that this was the place where Kaye stole the faces off the girls who had been here before them, before he murdered them quietly and medically in their beds and disposed of their bodies God knows how. But in the next second he realised that this room proved nothing of the kind. He had seen no bodies, no evidence of foul play. Everyone knew that Heat had an operating theatre in the house. This must be it.

But it felt bad. Were the bodies of dead, faceless girls and boys heaped up somewhere just out of sight?

'It's the operating theatre,' he said, and Sara gave him an odd, disbelieving glance that he simply could not interpret. Frantically he began twisting the lens this way and that, trying to find more – something that would finally disprove or prove for certain Sara's suspicions. Then, two things happened. From the corridor behind them came the sound of feet on the tiles; a group of people was approaching. Mark and Sara both squealed with surprise and stood up. At the same second a light was turned on in the room behind them; they could see the line of it under the door, lighting up the floor and their own feet. Someone was inside.

They were trapped. The feet in the corridor were growing louder by the second, and, to add to them, they could now hear footsteps from inside the room. Whoever was in there was coming towards the door. Mark made a dash for another door in the corridor, but it was too late. The locked door rattled and opened. A face looked out. It was Dr Kaye.

'You're early,' he exclaimed, seeing Sara. Then he looked at Mark and glared furiously. 'And what's he doing here?' he demanded.

Mark began to back off, but Sara just stood there. She seemed to have had the life sucked out of her. She stared at Kaye with her mouth open, her head to one side, a little frown on her face as if she was trying to understand what had just happened. Dr Kaye was scowling at them, but Mark could read nothing on his face to suggest that he'd been caught with his own terrible work behind him. He took Sara's hand and pulled her back. The jerk made her stagger backwards a couple of steps. But she didn't look at him at all. She had her eyes fixed on Kaye and began making small whimpering noises at the back of her throat. Then the approaching footsteps became suddenly loud as the people turned a final corner and came upon them. Mark and Sara turned and stood, hand in hand, to see who was going to emerge.

It was Jonathon Heat himself, accompanied by Tom Woods, a small of group of men and women in medical uniforms and the usual pack of bodyguards. When he turned the corner and saw them standing there together, Heat never paused in his movement, only speeded up slightly. Mark saw his eyes fixed on him like a snake's, and his head began to rock slightly from side to side, in rage or anxiety, perhaps. The footsteps rang out in the enclosed space, but Mark had an eerie impression that Heat was hissing slightly under his breath as he closed in. He showed no emotion.

'Hello, Mark,' he said in his mildest voice as he drew up

to them. 'What are you doing down here? This area is out of bounds to staff.'

Mark shrugged and glanced over at Kaye, then over and into the room. He felt that he had found them out, caught them red-handed, and yet what had he seen that could make any of these people guilty?

Heat looked at Sara, then to Mark, then to her again. Sara was standing there with a silly smile on her face. She lifted her hands up to cover her face, and Mark realised that it must have been the first time she had been bare-faced in front of so many people for weeks.

'Sara?' said Heat. 'Is Mark here with you?'

She nodded her head.

'I'm her boyfriend,' said Mark.

Heat looked at him through those half-hooded eyes and Mark thought, What the fuck are you thinking? What's going on in there, for God's sake? But Heat gave nothing away.

'That's not really my business,' he said at last. He looked at Sara. 'Are you ready now, Sara?' he said. 'They're waiting for us.'

She gave a funny little nod.

Mark licked his lips. What was going on? It was as if there was another life going on at the same time.

'She doesn't want the operation,' he told them. He moved closer to her and squeezed her hand. She seemed to have frozen. He had never seen her like this, that smile without meaning on her face. Her hand felt cold in his. She moved slightly away from him. He shook her hand urgently. He needed her to admit what they were doing here. It was time to stop pretending. 'She doesn't trust you,' he burst out. 'Stop playing games. We've seen everything. What are you going to do?' He glanced at Sara, willing her to own up and be on his side.

Or was it him she had been lying to all this time?

Heat didn't so much as flicker. 'I don't know what I'm going to do, Mark. Sack you, perhaps. I expect I'll take legal action for breach of trust, I don't know. But perhaps you'd better explain to me what you mean by saying you've seen everything? There are no secrets in this house.'

Mark jerked his head over his shoulder.

'There,' he croaked again, squeezing Sara's hand. She only needed to say! Why wouldn't she say?

Heat looked over his shoulder and into the room. His face gave nothing away. He walked round them into the room and gestured them after him. Mark and Sara stayed still, but the bodyguards grouped around and herded them after Heat into the room.

'There are no secrets here, are there, Sara? What, hasn't she told you, Mark? Sara knows this place, she's been here before, haven't you, Sara?' Sara nodded, smiling foolishly. 'This is the operating theatre, Mark. This is where the operation is to take place.'

Mark turned and stared at Sara, who had stopped smiling and was now looking puzzled.

'Did you know?' he asked her. Sara glanced away and frowned as if there was something she had forgotten that she was trying to remember.

'We were here earlier today, showing her round,' interrupted Dr Kaye. 'Not only that, but I've spent most of this evening assessing her and preparing her for this operation. I can't have my patients interfered with like this, it's ridiculous.' He glared at Heat, furious with this latest development. 'Maybe we should call the whole thing off – she's obviously been pulling the wool over our eyes.'

'Oh, no, not yours, Dr Kaye,' Sara cried out suddenly. Mark turned to her, but she pulled her hand away from his. She didn't seem to know where to turn. She put her hands up to the sides of her face and began to cry.

'Sara, we've been in meetings all day and I thought this was resolved. You know that all you have to do is say and we'll call it all off, but this really is your last chance. It's not fair on Jonathon. What do you say? Are we going ahead?' asked Kaye.

Sara wiped her nose on her arm, smiled bravely and said, 'Yes.'

Then everything moved very quickly. Woods stepped in between Sara and Mark, pushing Mark back towards the door, while Dr Kaye linked arms with Sara and led her deeper into the theatre.

'What are you doing? It's not time yet,' said Mark desperately.

'Sara's just in time, aren't you, Sara? The operation is tonight,' said Heat. He glared at Mark in a cold rage. 'If you've been taking advantage of this sick girl in the way I think you have, I'll have you run through the courts till you bleed, you sick bastard.'

A bodyguard stepped in. Suddenly Mark was being walked swiftly down the corridor by Woods and his men. He couldn't understand what was happening, but Sara looked so crushed, so hopeless – as if the presence of Kaye and Heat had sapped her of all her strength. He felt certain that she had somehow fallen into their power, although he had no idea how. Suddenly she was like someone else. And yet, from what they'd said, she'd known what the room was the whole time. Had she really agreed to this? Why was she playing such games with him? Even if she had agreed, it seemed to Mark that what they were doing to her was utterly without mercy.

They got him as far as the first corner. He was walking along in a daze, not understanding what had happened. Then he thought, Christ, what am I doing? Sara's in trouble, she needs me! He dug in his heels, flailed around at the bodyguard and started shouting, 'Sara! Sara! Come on – run for it.' And she responded – she came to the door – she got as far as that. She stood and looked at him. Mark dug his feet down and resisted the shoulders pushing into him, hurrying him along. He could actually hear Woods grinding his teeth in rage, but he stood firm. He could see Kaye standing behind Sara.

Suddenly she lifted her arms out to him, as if she was going to run and hug him, or as if she was pleading with him to take her with him. She let out a brief cry, like a bird. For a second, everything froze around him. Mark called her name and she took two rapid steps towards him; but immediately after his voice, like an echo, came Heat's calling her back.

She stopped, looked inside, back at Mark . . . then turned her head one last time and disappeared, of her own free will, back into the theatre. Mark never saw her again.

Now that they were out of sight, Woods and his crew stopped mucking around. They picked Mark up bodily and carried him. He stopped struggling. They were being much rougher than they needed to be and there was an implicit threat of real violence. They carried him to a white van parked behind the house. They dropped him to the ground and, as he got up, Woods punched him in the stomach so hard he fell at once, all the breath knocked out of him. Woods stood back and the three bodyguards grouped round him and kicked him around between them, quite casually, it seemed to him. No one said a word. It was very professionally done, Mark thought – nothing to the head or face, but he couldn't breathe without pain for days afterwards.

Woods bent down and frisked him as he lay on the ground, front and back, one of the bodyguards turning him over with his foot. Then they peeled him off the ground, flung him into the van and slammed the door on him. At the front, the doors opened and some people got in – he had no idea how many, the driving area was closed off from the back. There were muttered words between them and the men outside. Someone banged on the sides, the engine started up and he was driven off.

There were no windows, no cracks in the door where he might see out. Mark had no idea where he was being taken.

He tried to lever the door open with his fingers, but the van was new, well built and well locked. Heat and his men, their motives and plans and how far they were prepared to go to carry them out, were as big a mystery to him as ever. Detention, imprisonment or murder – he had no idea what was in store for him. And Sara! What was happening with Sara? Heat had said that she knew all along that that room was the operating theatre and she seemed to have admitted it; and yet her whole demeanour had been so confused and shocked, he couldn't believe she really knew or was in control of what was going on. She had seemed traumatised, but how could the discovery of something you already knew be traumatic? Mark felt disorientated and very frightened.

The operation had been brought forward. The layers of deceit and mystery surrounding the whole thing were getting thicker all the time. Even now, Sara was going under the knife.

As he put it himself later, 'I just wanted a second opinion.'

Mark tried shouting and yelling and banging on the plywood at the front of the van that separated him from the driver. After a minute of this the van pulled over and someone shouted to him.

'If I have to come back there, I won't stop kicking you until I hear the bones break. Understand? Don't think I'm joking.'

Mark knew he wasn't joking. He lay down on the floor and didn't dare make a sound.

The van took off again. Mark began to weep. All his care, all his efforts, all his planning, and he had failed to save her from anything.

It was about this time when he felt the Palm Pilot still in his inside pocket. At first he couldn't believe it. Could they have missed something so obvious? The video camera had been taken off him when they frisked him as he lay on the ground after his beating. But the Palm Pilot had escaped their hands.

Mark sat up as quietly as he could. The Palm Pilot was also a mobile phone. He had all his numbers still on it. But who to ring? The only person he could think of was Janet. He sat on the floor with his back to the panel, held his head in his hands, arms curled round him, so as to look in silent despair should his captors have a way of spying on him, and dialled her number.

There was no response. Sara had asked Janet to be available on the borrowed mobile to receive any calls she might make about a change of plans. Janet, anxious about her role, had turned her own off so as not to confuse matters.

He left a message, tried again, and again and again. Nothing.

Mark sat still in the van and wracked his brains. What could he do? Alert the police? To what? If he could think of nothing else, he would, but he had little hope of that succeeding. It seemed to him that everything was already lost. Nothing could stop the operation once it was under way, and who had the power to overcome someone like Jonathon Heat who could afford any level of help to achieve his ends?

In the end, he had one long shot left. There was one other person that he knew who did not like Heat, who despised Kaye and who, he knew, did not want Sara to go through with the operation. He'd met her once at dinner with Heat and Sara the day he arrived. He'd sometimes thought of contacting her, to try and find an ally, but she had been with Heat for so long that it seemed like a last resort. He had gone to the trouble of getting her mobile number off Sara though; and now he dialled it.

Bernadette.

Bernadette at the time was sitting in front of the television with a glass of brandy and hot water in her hand, fast asleep. Heat, as promised, had rung her shortly before nine and told her that so far, no decisions had been made. She didn't recognise Mark's voice, and when she first heard him breaking up over a bad signal she was inclined to put the phone impatiently down. But the word 'Sara' made her sit up in her chair and take notice. The crackly voice on the other end kept losing its signal and he had to ring back twice as the van sped in and out of range.

'Her boyfriend? But I didn't know she had one. Well!' Bernadette snorted. That girl! You couldn't tell what she was up to. Mark explained to her that the operation was taking place tonight.

'Now? No, you're wrong. Mr Heat told me himself that there was no decision until tomorrow morning.'

'No . . . now. They're doing it now. I saw them. I was there with her. Bernadette, she thinks he wants to steal her face.

Do you think that might be true?'

'No, no, no, I told you, Mr Heat himself said...'

'They took her in,' said Mark. 'They took me away and kicked the shit out of me. If he told you that, he's lying.'

Bernie sat up in her chair. 'How can you know?'

'I was there! Bernadette, I was there. You have to do something.'

A lie! Heat and his doctors had been sliding this way and that with their half-truths and evasions, bending things, twisting them so that they might or might not be true. Now here it was – a straight, cold, out-and-out lie. Yes! So now they had showed their true colours...

If it was true.

'They've got her right now. You have to stop them.'

'Wait there.'

'I'm not going anywhere.'

Bernadette rang off and phoned the house immediately. Heat's phone was turned off. Kaye's phone was turned off. She rang the staff, she had friends there yet. And it was confirmed. Her informant, one of the maids, was willing to speak against orders. Yes, it was true. The operation had already begun.

Heat had lied to her. It was like an avalanche. The medically cool assessments, the careful insistence on assent and professionalism – they were all a disguise. Heat was lying. The operation was not being put off – it was being brought forward. Bernadette herself – the child's nurse! – was being lied to. Murder, kidnap, everything was possible now. With a shriek she flung her hands into the air. What a fool she had been! The poor sick child had needed her, and she had come all the way across the Atlantic to sit in her chair and drink brandy while the knife was sinking in. Sara was in the hands of that dragon, that beast, that Bluebeard, that thief of souls and faces, Jonathon Heat. And she had allowed it to happen...

She picked up the phone, which she had dropped in her distress. 'I'll be back,' she snarled at the maid. Then she dialled the police.

Back in the van, Mark tried to ring Janet again but got no answer, so he rang Bernadette again – she was engaged too – and left her Janet's number. That was all he could do.

The van ran on into the night. His lovely Sara! He had tried to save her and failed.

He sat there with his back to the driver, hid his face down between his knees, and cried.

Sara's Face

'She thinks he wants to steal her face,' Mark had said. Just the idea of it drained all the energy and will out of Bernadette. It was so monstrous, so vile... But of course, so untrue. Heat was sick and Kaye was mad, but neither of them would play such a terrible trick, even if they thought they could get away with it. That wasn't the point. The point was, it was what Sara thought, and that in itself was a terrible confirmation of all that Bernadette feared. The girl was hopelessly unfit for cosmetic surgery of any kind, let alone having the knife range over almost the whole of her body, as Kaye was planning.

And, despite that, somehow between the two of them they had convinced her to enter the surgery with them.

Bernadette had been delayed, kept from her patient and ejected from the house. Promises had been made and then broken; she had been lied to by Heat himself. She didn't know exactly what was going on at Home Manor Farm, but she had let Sara down, she knew that much, and now she was determined to help her.

And what if it was true? Oh God – what if it was true!

Her first phone call was to the police. The name Jonathon Heat immediately attracted attention and she soon found herself trying to explain her fears to Inspector Derrick Alderson. Inspector Alderson listened carefully while Bernadette told him about the operation, about the lies Heat had told her, about Mark, kidnapped and kicked, and now held in a van going God knows where. Like many other people, he was appalled at what Heat had done to himself over the years, and was deeply suspicious of Wayland Kaye. But he had no reason to trust Bernadette and, even if he did, it was difficult to see what could be done about an operation that was already under way.

The minutes were ticking by. Bernadette was desperate.

'Ring the boy – you can do that, can't you? Ring everyone. Ring her mother, see if she knows what's going on, because no one else does, I can tell you that. Something's going on.' She took a breath and said the mad thing, the thing she feared was happening, and the thing she feared would make the police think she was a complete nutter.

'The boy says Sara thinks they want to steal her face.'

'Steal her face? How can they do that?'

'They can do that these days. It's that Dr Kaye – he can do anything. Really anything.'

There was silence on the other end of the phone.

'I'm not saying it's true,' begged Bernadette, trying very hard not to cry. 'I'm just saying that's what she thinks. Now a girl that thinks that, she shouldn't be going into surgery, should she? Don't you think, Inspector? Don't you?'

Bernadette ground to a halt, unable to speak.

'I'll look into it. We'll be in touch, Mrs McNalty.'

Bernadette put down the phone, put her head in her hands and cried. She had done what she could. Now it was in other hands than her own.

Inspector Alderson was at a bit of a loss as to how to proceed. His personal opinion was that it was all going to turn out to be a load of baloney, but if, on the other hand, there was anything in it at all, it would hit the press sooner rather than later and the police couldn't afford to be seen to be doing nothing. He put in a call to Home Manor Farm, where he got confirmation that yes, actually, an operation was taking place at that moment – very small, nothing much, a girl having some minor burn scars seen to and a few other bits and pieces. A little breast enhancement. The speaker wasn't sure what, exactly.

The girl's name was Sara Carter and she was seventeen years old. That made the inspector sit up a little. Seventeen was very young for such operations – and at Heat's house, and, yes, Dr Kaye was performing the op.

So much madness around one so young, thought the policeman. He put a couple of people on the case, to get in touch with the girl's mother and father, who surely ought to know what was going on, and to ring the boy Bernadette had mentioned, and to get the local force on the case. They could go round and check out the consent forms. It was worth having a look at this one, just out of curiosity if nothing else.

At last, at long last, a network was rising up to help Sara. But so, so late! Even now, Dr Kaye was peeling away the flesh, while his assistant prepared Heat to receive her beauty. Despite her madness, it was all exactly as Sara feared.

Mark had been taken at about half past ten. It was about 11.15 when he received a call from the police. Fortunately, he'd had the sense to put his phone on vibrate. In a quiet voice, he confirmed what Bernadette had said – yes, the operation had been brought forward at short notice; yes, Sara had been planning on leaving; yes, she was frightened that they were going to steal her face. No, there was no evidence. But she was seeing ghosts in there! No one in their right mind would put such a vulnerable girl through any sort of cosmetic procedures, surely?

The van passed out of signal, but Mark had said his piece. Something was happening, at least, but as far as he could tell, it was already too late. He assumed that the minor procedures they planned would be almost finished by now. He did not know that they were actually removing her face even as he spoke.

It was roughly half past twelve by the time the van pulled off the motorway and into traffic. From what Mark could gather, it was a town – there were plenty of stops and starts and quite a bit of traffic, considering the hour. He suspected they were in London. They must be nearing their destination. The van moved on, slowly now, and over a bumpy road – obviously not London after all.

The van pulled up; the men got out. The door opened. Mark was gestured to come out. He had no particular plan and no idea what they were going to do with him – desert him, question him, beat him or kill him. His fear that he would make things worse for himself, his natural good manners and sheer unfamiliarity with threat and violence all made it difficult for him to act, but he managed it. It was pathetic really – he was aware of it at the time. He was small, out of condition and untrained; the two men were big, fit and trained. Nevertheless, as he stood in front of one and with his back to the other, Mark thought that he had to try. He'd already been frozen once when Sara walked away into the operating theatre. He didn't want that to happen again.

So he kicked the one in front of him in the balls.

To his amazement, it worked. The man doubled up with a breathy groan. Mark stood staring down at him writhing at his feet in amazement; then the man behind him grabbed his neck. Mark jerked his head back, more to try to see what was going on than anything else, and by sheer good luck caught the man in the nose with the back of his head. The man yelped and let him go. Mark ran for it, the man with the bloody nose on his heels. He could actually hear him snarling through bubbles of blood.

He was as good as dead now, even if he hadn't been before.

He knew at once he had no chance of escaping from his pursuer, who was bigger, stronger, fitter and faster. After ten steps the feet were right on his heels; he could almost feel the hands reaching out for him. So he stopped running and curled up in a ball on the ground. The man tripped over him. Mark got up and ran away again in the opposite direction.

Behind him, the man got up after him and the chase began again.

No one had made a sound – maybe there were people nearby, but that didn't occur to Mark until later; all he wanted to do was hide where he couldn't be found. After another twenty steps he was completely out of breath and the man was again almost on his back. Mark had exhausted his repertoire of fight tricks, so he did the same thing again – curled up in a ball. To his amazement it worked; again the man tripped over him, again Mark got up and ran away. The man got up and followed him, all in quietness. It was like a slapstick sequence out of the old silent movies. To one side, Mark could see the other man beginning to straighten up and hobble towards him and he knew he had to get away properly or they would get him between them. He still couldn't think of any new tricks, however, so he did the old one again: curling up in a ball. It worked – the man must have thought no one could possibly be so stupid as to try that again. Down he went with a cry this time. Mark was so out of breath he could hardly move, but he got up and hobbled onwards, doubled up with a stitch, gasping for breath and with a red mist of exhaustion before his eyes. This time, there were no feet after him. He risked a glimpse back. His pursuer was on his feet but hobbling badly. Mark's luck had held – the man had obviously hurt his foot in that final fall. He was almost incoherent with rage and started shouting and bawling at Mark to come back. The man with the kicked crotch was also on the move, so Mark gathered up the last of his strength, and ran off into the darkness.

After a short dash he came to a heap of rubbish – it was dark and he couldn't see well, but it looked like bin bags and bits of wood and other stuff. In fact, he had been taken to a municipal tip. Behind, his pursuers were on the move. The rubbish heap was steep and Mark had no energy left to climb it, so instead, he did the only thing he could do – he dug a hole in it about a metre up, climbed inside and covered himself over with rubbish.

Seconds later, they arrived on the spot. They took a few faltering steps up the rubbish heap and paused. One of them was actually standing on his head.

'Where the fuck's he gone?'

'Up there somewhere, he must be.'

'How's he got up there? This stuff's all over the place, we'd hear him.'

It was true; the rubbish was unstable. If he was up there, they'd hear him. The other man took a couple of steps up and stood on Mark's feet. He felt like a dead man with the angels top and bottom.

The two men began to argue about what to do. One of them went back to get a torch while the other scouted around the tarmac area around the tip. But the game was already over, and Mark knew it. They'd left the spot where he lay; they'd not find him again. All he had to do was to stay still, keep mum and hope they didn't come back that way.

After what seemed like hours, the men left. Mark waited for ages – hours perhaps – before he came out; they could be waiting for him, how could he tell? He emerged into pitch darkness. He phoned the police and left his number with the operator. Then he buried himself again in the rubbish and more or less passed out.

Meanwhile, the police investigation was gathering momentum. They had discovered that Jessica did not know that the operation was taking place that night. They had also been examining their records and discovered that Heat had answered questions before about a young girl in trouble. It wasn't much, but it tied in. She had disappeared two years previously and had never been seen since. Her last known job and place of residence were Home Manor Farm, where she had been employed as a housemaid. Her name was Catherine Monroe. Finally, the man who had gone out to the house to examine the consent papers was being stalled. The papers had been misplaced, apparently. All in all, it was beginning to look to Inspector Alderson as if something fishy was going on.

At midnight, another, less official front swung into operation, this time put into motion by Sara herself. As the pips sounded, Janet fulfilled her promise to her friend. She had no idea that Sara had gone into the operation after all – she had not picked up her own mobile all evening out of a nervous dread of being traced somehow to these calls she was about to make. But she was determined to do her bit. Nervously, she dialled a number and spoke to a local news desk. After the first one, she moved on to a couple of other locals, then to a well-known daily. It was getting easier. Soon she was on to a staff reporter on *Heat* magazine, then on to

OK, NOW, the *Daily Mirror*, the *Sun* and so on. Sara had been as good as her word – the password, 'Sara's Face', made them all jump to attention – Janet could hear it in their voices. Rapidly, a small army of overexcited reporters, cameramen and news crews jumped into their cars and vans and sped off through the night to Home Manor Farm. They didn't know quite what was going on, but Jonathon Heat had been teetering on the edge of total disaster for years now. Sara had promised them the news story of their lives. They were prepared to risk life, limb and integrity to get it.

Before long, the front gate was a blaze of TV lights. Images of Home Manor Farm, where a young fan was rumoured to be being subjected to facial surgery she had not consented to – surgery performed by Heat's notorious surgeon, Dr Wayland Kaye – were being broadcast in every country in the world. There were even rumours that Heat was in the process of stealing her face.

Of course, at this point, no one really believed it, but that was irrelevant. News isn't about what's true, but about whether journalists can find someone who thinks it might be; an accusation is true enough. In this case, Sara's mother, Jessica, didn't know the operation was taking place at that time, Bernadette had been promised it wasn't happening at that time and Sara's friend Janet, who of course the press were in touch with within the hour, claimed that Sara had actually been planning on running away before they ever touched her. It was enough. Anyway, even if it wasn't true, it ought to be as far as the magazines were concerned. They had been after Kaye for years. The mere fact that he was operating on a seventeen-year-old girl was enough to make the headlines.

The combination of press and police acted like an explosive. The investigation was turned up. The consent papers, when the police finally got their hands on them after much delay and obfuscation by the Heat household, had the wrong date and the exact nature of the operation Sara was undergoing was unclear to say the least. By this time, the investigation was out of the hands of Inspector Alderson; the Chief Constable of Cheshire was on the case. At 1 a.m. the police requested permission to enter the operating theatre to check that everything was as Heat's household claimed it was. Permission was refused. They were now told that there were complications. Sara had reacted badly to the anaesthetic and Dr Kaye was fighting for her life. At 3 a.m. the operation was still under way and the extraordinary decision was made to seek an injunction to enter the operating theatre and make sure nothing untoward was going on.

Things were now moving very fast indeed. In the heat of the investigation and the hysteria of the press interest, it came out that Heat had asked Sara to fill in a form that allowed her organs to be used for transplant if anything should happen to her. Her heart, her liver – why not her face? Still no one believed it, but no satisfactory reasons were being given to keep independent doctors and surgeons out of the operating theatre and at 7 a.m., a policeman, in company with no less than four eminent doctors, knocked at the front door armed with the injunction to enter the theatre and even to stop the operation if necessary. Sara and her face had been put into the care of the courts. She had now been in surgery for over eight hours.

The policeman knocked; the flashlights popped. The door opened. The household had been warned, but seemed to be doing their best to slow the whole thing down as much as possible. The policeman was asked to wait. He shook his head. An argument ensued. The policeman stood to one side, waved his hand behind him and ten heavy officers pushed their way into the house.

Down in the basement, where Heat had built the private operating theatre, the latest operation was going according to plan. It seems likely that Kaye and Woods felt that the further the operation went, the harder it would be to stop it. Only half an hour before, Sara's face had been plucked up from the front of her head and laid neatly on the bloodied front of Heat's. There had as yet been no time to connect any nerves, but to move things further on, Kaye had stitched it on at the tip of his nose. Sara, meanwhile, lay unconscious, paralysed, faceless and expressionless under a sheet, a layer of sterilised tissue over her face to keep the wounds fresh. The remains of Heat's face had already been removed and incinerated.

The police entered as the surgeon was putting in the last stitches on the nose. There was no shouting in theatre with such delicate work going on, but Tom Woods was hissing in the senior officer's ear, demanding that he leave. Kaye himself seemed relieved. He flung down his knife and walked out, pulling off his rubber gloves without saying a word. His juniors began the work of stabilising the faces of the two patients; there would be a wait before Sara could be taken away. Already, counter-claims against the injunction were under way; it could still be reversed.

And reversed it was within the hour, with the surgeons still preparing the two patients to wait for further surgery. An hour after that, the injunction was again put in place and three hours after the police had entered the house, Sara and Heat were removed from the house into a crowd of yelling, shoving journalists. Both were unconscious, and both would remember it in years to come not from their own senses but from the endless photographs and video footage of the scene – the police crowding round, the emergency vehicles waiting on the gravel, the flashing lights, the two trolleys with the patients – victims? – clients? – being wheeled into separate ambulances. There was a frightful moment when one of the dogs, badly trained, or perhaps spooked by the crowd, or tempted by the smell of blood, leaned to one side and snatched at the sheet covering one of the bodies. The cameras snapped and rolled, and revealed to the world the now famous image of Sara's face, inert in a way no face ever should be. But it wasn't Sara who was wearing it – it was Heat himself.

The question now was – who owned Sara's face?

Epilogue: Lucy Smith

It's a lovely drive through the Berkshire countryside, all rolling pastures and hedgerows. It's where I grew up. For such a heavily populated county, there's a lot of woodland. I live in the north now, where people tend to think of the southern fields and woods as being too neat, too ordered. They love the moors and the rocky places, the crags and the big skies. I love them, too, but it's the green valleys and beech woods that touch me inside as only a homecoming can.

Berkshire has its rough side, same as everywhere else, but it also has far more than its fair share of rich people and places. Actors, rock stars and other celebrities buy hidden farmhouses next to wealthy aristocrats. The land is fertile, the place has been rich for centuries. There's the river Thames flowing fatly along past green pastures, boating houses, long gardens with a jetty on the end and pretty villages and towns. It's *Three Men in a Boat* country. On the downs, they breed racehorses.

Berkshire attracts more than its fair share of horsey people, too. There are riding stables, stud farms, racecourses. It was to visit the owner of one of those stud farms that I was going today. Her name is Lucy Smith.

You won't have heard of her – not yet anyway.

Some explanation is called for here.

The events I'm about to describe took place in April 2006, more than a month after I'd finished this book. That is to say, after I thought I'd finished this book. I'd been invited by the company who had commissioned me to write the story to come to the stud farm and talk to Lucy, who, I was told, had some information that would cast a new light on the story so far.

I was intrigued. I was also annoyed – I'd already finished the wretched thing, I was on to something new. I don't like going over old ground and I was unsure about how much more work was going to be involved. What if I had to rewrite the whole book?

But I was also intrigued. I knew as much as anyone else alive about Sara and her strange story, and yet here was someone I'd never even heard of who was apparently in possession of important information. What did she know? Who was Lucy Smith, and what was her relationship to Sara?

The fact was, it was an offer I just couldn't refuse. As Lucy must surely have known.

I was a little early – she was still out on her ride, the stable manager told me – so I waited in the yard and watched the comings and goings. Busy places, stables. All very nice, very ordered out there in the pretty countryside – but there's something rather urban about them. Perhaps it's because horses used to be a means of transport and there would have been so many more in the towns once, same as cars today. And the clothes people wear – there's something a little military about them. It's not quite, but almost a uniform.

The horses were lovely – beautiful big beasties, some chestnut, some black, but most of them that less elegant spotted and splashed mixture of colours that horses often are – friendly-looking colours. The stable hands were brushing down a shaggy red mare, mucking out, wandering to and fro about God knows what jobs – horsey people always seem to be doing something. Someone led one clopping over the concrete and along a short track to a training ring. In a field beyond, there was a handful of mares and their foals, and next to them a couple of huge shire horses nibbling at a bundle of hay hanging from a tree, two metres off the ground. Lucy took an interest in several different breeds, it seemed.

Caring for animals seems like a nice way to make some money – not that there was much of a shortage of that around here. Birds sang, there was the distant sound of a tractor at work. I found it difficult to imagine that this was where the story I had been writing over the past months had ended up.

A rider came down the track, a chalky, flinty little road with a hawthorn hedge on either side. She sat very upright, wore a neat black hard hat and jodhpurs – all the correct gear. It looked out of place. After all, she was out riding for pleasure, she didn't need to dress up for it.

I gave her a little wave just to show who I was – as if she didn't know – but she rode right in without casting me so much as a glance. One of the stable boys came to take the horse by the bridle as she dismounted, although she seemed an excellent rider; she hardly seemed to need help. She stroked the horse, patted his neck. Then she threw her arms suddenly round his face and loved him. The stable boy waited patiently until she was done, took the bridle off her and led the horse away to be brushed and groomed. Lucy watched them leave, disappointed, I think, that she wasn't going to do it herself. Or perhaps disappointed that she now had an unpleasant job to do instead. She put her hands on her hips in a defiant gesture and, as the horse bent to drink outside the stable door, at last half turned her head and gave me a sideways look.

I waved again. She paused, sighing perhaps. She twisted her head slightly in acknowledgement and walked across to meet me.

We shook hands. There was the scent of almonds and musk and on her cheek, pale and new and covered with a layer of make-up, I could make out the triangular burn the iron had left there over a year before.

'I guess you don't want to be doing this,' I said.

Her eyes went to one side, thinking about it. But she didn't answer.

'We can talk over here,' she said, nodding to a set of tables and benches set out under a group of beech trees behind the stable. As we went past one of her employees, she asked for drinks to be brought over to us.

'It's a lovely place here, just gorgeous,' I told her as we sat down. Lucy frowned at the table and, disconcertingly, answered the previous thing I'd said.

'I must want to do it, or I wouldn't be doing it, I suppose,' she said.

'But why should you do it? You don't seem all that happy about it,' I said, and I laughed although I'd said nothing funny, to soften the statement.

Lucy shrugged. 'I think I must want my story to be told. We all do, don't we? Want people to know what it was like, what happened.'

'Right. So tell me!'

She tipped back her head; under her jawline I could see the operation scar. Of course, I was watching her face all the time for signs of damage. You'd never guess that it had made a journey away from her and back again. But it was somewhat immobile. She had lost some movement. Her lower lip hung rather limp. Bizarrely, it really was now a kind of living mask.

Or perhaps she was just keeping her feelings to herself.

'The trouble is, I've no idea,' she admitted. 'There's whole chunks I can't remember. It's like it happened to someone else – in fact, it did happen to someone else. But I know what it felt like.' She pulled her stiff face into something of a smile. 'You'll have to make do with that.'

I smiled back. The drinks arrived. I sipped my tea and watched her watching me over the top of her glass.

'OK, then. In your own words? Do you know what you want to say?'

'Here and there. No, you start. Ask me a question. It's your job, isn't it?'

'I write novels normally. This is new to me. OK, for starters, why did you ask me to do this? You could have had anyone.'

Lucy smiled. 'I like your books. I read them back then, you know. I was reading *Lady* in that last week in Jonathon's house. You make things up, but they're still true. That seemed sort of appropriate somehow.'

I felt flattered, but I wasn't at all sure of how to do this. I'd never done this sort of thing before. Probing people – that's the job of an interviewer, isn't it? This whole story was full of dodgy people doing dodgy things; Lucy was one of them.

I did another easy one: why was she all dressed up to go riding? Was it a special event?

Lucy laughed. 'There's always been a way to look, a way to dress. That hasn't changed. I like the clobber,' she said, and she stretched her arm and tugged at the neat black sleeves of her jacket. 'I luuuurrve the clobber.' She relaxed and took off her hat and jacket, propped her chin on her elbows. 'Go on, then. Is that the best you can do?'

'Well, yes. I'm nervous,' I admitted. 'So, OK. What about the name, then? You changed your name. What was wrong with Sara?'

She tipped her head back and laughed. 'What wasn't wrong with Sara? She was all over the place. New life. New name. New me.' She spread her hands and smiled, like she was a magician.

'But *is* it all new? Isn't it still you?'

She rested her chin on her hands, looked at me and gently shook her head.

'One thing you should understand, something I should say before we go any further,' she said. 'I'm not Sara. Sara's dead. She never came out of the anaesthetic.' She looked at me to see how I was going to take this piece of news. 'We share the same . . .' She gestured down at her body. 'I mean, it's me, but not like that. Not like her. When I woke up after the op I wasn't the same. For a long time I thought I'd turn back into myself but I never did. Sara's gone. She really did die.'

And was she sorry about that?

'Sorry, yes, I suppose I am really. She was a piece of work, wasn't she, Sara? But, you know, she wasn't a particularly good person or a nice person, even though she was so special. She was marvellous . . .' She smiled proudly, rather in the way Janet smiled when she was talking about her. 'If she'd lived, maybe she'd have grown up and turned into someone good. Someone real. But I'm happier like this.' She nodded; she was very clear about that. 'I know who I am like this.'

'You say you were expecting to wake up and be yourself again. That seems to say that you knew who you were all along.' I paused. I wasn't sure how to ask my question. 'The thing is, I spoke to all those people, and you were telling so many different stories. You were telling Heat and Kaye one thing, Mark another, Janet still another thing. I sometimes got the feeling you were making everything up, and sometimes I got the feeling it was all real to you, in different ways. So what was real? Did you . . . I mean, did Sara know what was real and what wasn't?'

'Right.' She laughed. 'The thing about Sara is...back then...I don't think she really believed in real. It was just stories to her. I don't think it even occurred to her whether they were real or not real. How well they fitted in, how well they worked – she liked all that. She loved all that. But that was about it. I don't think any one thing was more real than the other.'

'Even right up to having your face off?'

'Even right up to that.'

'What about the ghost, the apparition? Was that real?'

'Well, it was real, wasn't it? Mark heard it, too, didn't he?'

'Well, sort of. Do you know what he said? He said, "Sometimes, I think the screaming in Sara's head was so loud, I could hear it, too."'

She laughed, delighted. 'He said that? He used to say wonderful things – you have no idea. Maybe he was right. What about the blood on my sleeve that time? Did you ask him about that?'

'He saw it. But he was never sure you didn't put it there yourself.'

'Maybe I did. I can't ever really remember...' She smiled. I got the feeling she liked not remembering everything.

'Really?' I said.

'Why should you believe me? But yes, really.'

'So the ghost was real...'

'It was real. The question is, who was it?'

'That was going to be my next question,' I said.

We smiled. Now she was conducting her own interview.

'So. You or Katie? Who was it?'

Sara paused. 'I have an opinion on that,' she said. 'But it is just an opinion.'

'Go on, then.'

'Katie.'

'Heat was cleared of any charges except the ones against you.'

'But they never found her, did they? She disappeared. No charges doesn't mean nothing ever happened. Listen, I'll tell you something.' She leaned forward. 'On that last day at Home Manor Farm, I had a final meeting with Dr Kaye, remember that?'

'Yes, and you came back in tears.'

'That's right. I've never told anyone the real reason for that. While I was waiting in his office, he had to leave for some message or other. While he was gone I looked through a folder on his desk. And guess what I found?'

I shrugged. I had no idea.

'Photos of girls, four or five of them. I was one. Katie was another.'

'I see.' I didn't know what to say. I was shocked. The implications of that were appalling. 'That never came out in court, did it?'

She gestured impatiently. 'The lawyers didn't let me testify, you know that. My evidence was discounted because my memory was so shot. But that's what happened. I reckon Heat and Kaye had stolen the faces of more than one other person. I reckon that was the secret of Dr Kaye's success. He just kept giving Heat a new face until, in the end, the nerves and the blood vessels gave up. And I'll tell you something else. That mask he used to wear. I reckon it was made of Katie's skin.'

She leaned back. She looked exhausted. I was horrified. 'Do you really believe that?' I asked her.

Lucy's expression had been hard and determined a moment before, but now her face fell. 'I don't really know, is the truth,' she said softly, and she looked so sad as she said it.

'OK, then.' I looked through my notes for another question. Lucy watched me, smiling ruefully. 'That Sara!' she exclaimed. 'You couldn't trust a word she said.'

'Tell me about Mark,' I asked her.

'God, I loved that boy.' She looked away; she was upset. 'I loved him so much. When I woke up and everything had changed...I'd changed...I was heartbroken, really. I suppose love is a story, too, isn't it? And I knew it had ended.' Again, the little shrug as if to say – what can you do?

'Why did you never see him again? He was heartbroken, too, you know.'

'I know.' She shook her head as if she couldn't believe her own life. 'But if I went back to him...what if it all started again? Sara was getting so scared as the operation came closer and closer. Poor Mark, he did everything he could to rescue her.'

'They all did.'

'They all did. I know, I know.' She shook her head. 'I can't go back. I can't see any of them ever again. I'm myself now. Maybe she isn't dead, maybe she's just asleep. What about that? She was such a terrifying person to be. If I see him again, maybe she'll wake up. I admired Sara, she was so wonderful, her head was so full of a million things. She was talented and marvellous and I'm just ordinary. But she was terrifying. I think to myself, Let her lie. I'm sorry about it. I think of them all a lot – Janet, Bernie – she was great, wasn't she? Even my mum. But I don't even like talking about them, not really. Most of the time I try not to even think about them, to be honest.'

I touched my chest. In my pocket I had a letter for her from Mark. Part of the conditions I'd had to sign to speak to her was that I wouldn't let anyone know where she was. But when I'd talked to him, he'd handed me a letter.

'Just in case,' he said. It was important to him. But something, made me hang back. Not yet, I thought, not yet ...

'You say she loved him, and you say Sara's dead. But you have feelings for him, still.'

Lucy – Sara, I was certain she was still Sara – stared at me. 'That's not how I think about it,' she said in an unsteady voice. 'You know, it's all stories, everything we do, everything we remember – Sara was right about that. But you have to think it's real. Yes, I have feelings for him but I want to let her lie, do you see?' She glanced from side to side at the table and chairs, at her own hands, as if the whole thing would suddenly dissolve and turn to paste if she stopped thinking about it right.

'She's the past,' she said. 'That's how I have to think about her.'

I nodded. Time to change the subject.

'OK. So... all right. What about this? Janet told me how Sara could make people up out of thin air – you sounded like a magician when she talked about it. Is Lucy someone Sara made up?'

She stared at me. 'I don't remember being there at the same time as her. Maybe she did make me up. But then she forgot herself...'

Curious! And yet, as the interview went on, her habit of talking about Sara as 'she' slipped, and she became 'me' more and more.

'Can we talk about Jonathon Heat?'

'Go on.'

'You can always say no if you don't like the question.'

'Go on, then.'

'Well – what do you think of him? Was he a monster? Or was he a victim? No one seems to know.'

Sara stared at the horses, their heads sticking out of the stables. A couple of them looked back at her. She spent a bit of time thinking about that one. She sighed. 'Both, I suppose. Same as me. All those things he had done to himself.'

'Do you feel sorry for him?'

She shook her head. 'Nope.'

'In the trial, he said he had no idea what Kaye was doing. Is he telling the truth, do you think?'

'Nope. He knew, he knew all along.' She paused as if she was going to say more, but then shrugged slightly again.

'Do you hate him?' I asked.

'Hate? No. I don't hate him or Kaye. This is a good life.'

'But you lost your face.'

245

'I got it back,' she said, looking at me.

'Did you? Not everything.'

I felt I was being a bit brutal, but she didn't flinch.

'Yes, I lost a lot of movement. But I could have lost a lot more than that. And in a sense, you know, I did it to myself.' She stopped and looked at me.

'Go on,' I said. 'What do you mean?'

I waited. She seemed to be considering. The thing was, maybe this was to do with the real question – the big question, the one I hadn't asked yet. The question, Why? Why did she go back into the operating theatre when everything was set up for her to escape – when Heat and Kaye offered her the chance of walking away? Why do that?

She gave me her stiff little smile and told me this story...

In the late afternoon before that last night Heat came to her room to let her know what was going on and, for the first and last time, Sara let him sleep with her. She allowed him at last into her big four-poster bed, drew the curtains and made love with him.

'It was the last time I was going to see him,' she told me. 'And, you know, it wasn't like my feelings for Mark, but I did love him.'

Afterwards they curled up among the rumpled sheets and had the following conversation. He was lying with his back to her and she was stroking his shoulder. She had the words on her lips for a long while, and hesitated to utter them because she felt that, if she did, they might become real.

'Jonathon,' she said. 'Will you make me a promise?'

'Anything,' said Jonathon, lifting his hand to place it on hers.

'Promise me that whatever happens, no one will be allowed to let me die.'

There was a pause; then he turned over to look at her. He didn't answer her, just looked into her eyes.

'What a question,' he said.

'Do you promise?'

'Of course I promise,' said Heat. 'I don't need to, though...' And he paused, unsure about where this was going.

'Am I pretty?' said Sara at last.

'Oh, come on!'

And then she said – and this is in her own words – 'Would you like my face?'

Heat gave a sharp intake of breath; she was speaking the unspoken. Then there was a long pause, in which, as Sara understood it, 'He knew that I knew and I knew that he knew...'

Heat looked away for a moment. Then he said, 'I would give anything to have your face, Sara, you know that.'

'Anything? How much is anything?'

'Half my kingdom?' he suggested, and she believed that there was the hint of a smile under his mask.

'Only half?'

'All of it, then.'

Sara looked away and sighed. 'You know, if I gave you my face it wouldn't be for money. It'd be for love.'

'You love me?' he asked. 'Are you sure?'

'Not you! I love your name. I love your fame. I love what you've done.'

'Then you do love me,' said Heat. Another pause. 'If you gave me your face, you'd need money.'

'I suppose.'

He reached out and stroked her cheek.

'And what would happen to me?' asked Sara.

'You'd be like this,' said Heat, and he lifted up his mask. Underneath was flesh and bone and blood and little else. He waited while she had a good look at the ruin, then he pulled it back down.

'At least until we found you a donor. It could be a long time. You and I match, our tissues match. It doesn't happen often. But we'd find someone, in the end.'

'And then?' I asked.

Lucy smiled. 'I said I'd think about it.'

I was incredulous. 'You wanted to give him your face. That's unbelievable!'

'I think I was trying to trap him when I started out. That's why I slept with him.'

'Christ. But then – were you intending to go in there at that point?'

'I don't think so.'

'Then for God's sake, why? Why did you go in there if you knew what was going to happen?'

Sara touched her face, with its red triangle from the iron still stamped to her. It was like a print – you could see the marks under the make-up where the holes were to let the steam through.'

'I used to hurt myself, did you know that?' She rolled up her sleeves. There were thin white lines over the inside of her elbows. 'Here, too. Although I did that so it couldn't be seen.' She smiled. 'Such a calculating cat!'

'Are you saying you went into the theatre like that – to hurt yourself?'

'She went in ... for all sorts of reasons. For one thing,' said Lucy, 'I never felt it was me. This.' She tapped her face. 'I always felt I was inside, looking out through my eyeholes. I'd look in the mirror and think, This isn't me. In some ways, you know, Dr Kaye was right. It almost felt that having my face off would let me out – the real me, the me I want to be. The me I am now, for instance; I'm real at last,' she said. She looked straight at me for the first time and gave me a smile that, despite the stiffness of her face, I can only call dazzling.

I was about to ask her another question but she ploughed on.

'And Sara achieved her aim – she's so famous now, isn't she? She gave away her face and then won it back. All those pictures of her. She could have a career in celebrity.' She laughed as she used those words. 'Any time she wants. And she made things different, didn't she? The difference between giving and being robbed, she confused it. Being famous. What you look like. She made people think, didn't she? She achieved what she wanted to achieve. She became a kind of event, an artwork. But, yes, she liked to hurt herself, too. Perhaps she even wanted to die. She did die. She had to die.

She was too much.'

'So . . . were you not planning on going away with Mark at all, then?'

'Oh yes, I was planning that. Absolutely. I . . . she, she had a lot of plans. She just didn't know which one was real until the moment came. Sara was one of those people who could believe in more than one thing at the same time.'

'I see.' I looked through my notes for more questions. I felt that she had struck me dumb.

'The operating room . . .' I said.

'Right. The funny thing is, I knew all about the operating theatre all the time. They'd taken me there and showed it to me several times. I'd been there that same day. But then, like, with Mark I knew nothing about it at all. I was really surprised when Kaye opened the door and there it was. No, not surprised – horrified. Terrified. I thought, I know this. I know it! And then it all slotted into place and I knew then, I really was mad. That's how sick I was. I could know things and not know them at the same time. That's bonkers, isn't it? I mean, seeing ghosts and spending all that time trying to get behind a door when you know about it all the time. That's when I decided to go ahead with it.'

'Right then? As late as that?'

'That's right.' She nodded. 'That late. Up to then, anything could have been real. All the things I was telling them, all the plans I was making, they were all just tests. I think I was waiting to discover which was the real version. But then I realised that Kaye must be right all along, and I went for it.'

She glanced down at her watch. I smiled.

'You can't tell me your whole story in half an hour, you know,' I protested.

'I couldn't tell my story in a hundred years. You know what my story is? My story is that I don't know either.'

I ducked my head. 'Maybe Sara's not so dead after all,' I suggested.

'Maybe,' she said, without a flicker. 'I wouldn't know.'

I looked at her. 'Are you trying to say you've had enough?'

She smiled. 'I did say I'd just answer a few questions.'

'OK. Coupla tabloid questions? I'm afraid I get just as curious as everyone else.'

'Go on.'

'Boyfriend?'

'Private,' she said.

'Why did you sleep with Heat?'

She smiled grimly. 'He was doing so much for me, it seemed the least I could do.' And she laughed, amused at her own antics. I smiled back.

'Anything to add on that subject?'

She shook her head.

'I guess we're almost done,' I said.

She leaned back in her chair.

'One last one – may I? Just curious. That last day – before Heat came to see you – you were on your own for a few hours. It was almost the only time you spent on your own in that house. What did you do?'

'Well, you know what? I've wondered myself. I don't know. I've tried to remember but' – she tapped her head – 'she won't

251

tell me.' I must have looked puzzled because she laughed at me. 'You're a novelist, you're used to the mystery being solved, a proper ending with everything tied up. But this is real life. The mystery remains, the end isn't finished, and there you are thinking that if you just imagine it hard enough or ask the right question . . . Bang!' She clapped her hands. 'It all comes real.' She looked triumphantly at me as she clapped her hands, as if a continent would spring up on the table top in front of me, or the whole thing, the table and drinks, the horses, ourselves, the fields and the Berkshire woods, would all drift away like a veil of coloured dust.

'Finished?' she asked.

I thought about it. She'd told me nothing was real, that everything was real, that she had been both cured and murdered. Surely that was enough.

'Finished,' I said. 'So.' I pulled a face. 'Now I have to rewrite the whole thing, I suppose.'

'Oh, no. Don't do that. I like what you've done; I don't want you to change a word. Just put me in . . . as an epilogue. That's all I really am. An epilogue to Sara's life.'

I nodded. Why not? It was her story, after all.

She smiled as widely as she could and spread her arms.

'Do you ride? Would you like a gallop?'

'I never learned.'

'Pity. It's the best thing. Horses! I love 'em! Well! Isn't this lovely?'

She stretched her arm out at the hedges and the horses, at the woods beyond. It certainly was lovely. She smiled at me. I smiled back.